NOWHERE, EVERYWHERE:
A Good Place to be From

by Josie Blaine

It was one of those sunny spring days at the cusp of summer in North Dakota, when not one of the thirty-one high school seniors could concentrate on Mr. Anderson's
U. S. History lecture. Gertrude was listening. She really was hearing, with her droopy eyes occasionally glancing at Mr. Anderson. The warmth of the April afternoon rays through the window was hitting her desktop, creating a perfect square of sunlight and making it hard for her to focus any longer on the influx of the immigrants in the Nineteenth Century. What had the lion's share of her attention was out the window.

Two of last year's senior boys, Spencer and Billy Ray, were climbing around on the roof of Grandpa Christiansen's house across the street from school. Spencer planned on marrying Mary Schultz this summer, and that would be their house. Spencer and Mary had been going out together all through high school, so it was a given they would have a June wedding. Mary was going to be a teacher, just like she'd planned to be since she'd set up a teddy bear and porcelain doll classroom in her bedroom in third grade. She would be off to Mayville this fall at the Teacher's College. Spencer would miss her, but he would be working hard at the lumber mill and the rail yard, and saving up as much money as he could, and fixing up that house.

Working at the lumberyard and in the rail yard would afford Spence cheap lumber for his fix-up projects on the home, and when Mary was finished with college in a year, she would come home and teach. It would be awfully convenient to live across the street from the school. Mary would be the teacher who would light the woodstove to warm the school in the mornings. The nearest teacher to the school these days was Mrs. Thompson, and Gertie thought she had to be getting toward seventy. Mrs. Thompson struggled up School Hill every morning to open the schoolhouse. What dedication, Gertie Thought.

Mary would be home on Christmas break, and her schooling would be finished in a year. Until then, Spencer would be putting this house in working order, awaiting his bride's return. Bachelor life would not be all that difficult for him, as his mother and sisters would still be cooking for him. Mary was the one who had to go away from her world, and be truly independent, Gertrude thought.

Gertrude wondered about college. Some girls went to the Teacher's College, then worked as teachers and got married and stopped working for good, or for a while, and had children. She really thought it sounded fun when she heard the stories from some of her older friends, returning for the summer break. Her friends who had gone on to the teachers' school spent a lot of time getting to know other girls, and learning about more than just math and history. There was a boys' school in a nearby town, and wouldn't you just know it, those boys would come around, looking for dates to the social events. Dances were held at either college on holidays, and Gertrude heard of some of the girls dressing as flappers. That sounded like a whole lot of fun. She wanted to dress up and shine. She wanted to be colorful and she wanted to be pretty and have everyone look at her and maybe even have a few boys flirt with her. Gertrude looked down at her brown, farm girl shoes and absentmindedly reached up and twirled a golden red curl on her shoulder, and figured those kind of fantasies were not for dairy barn girls. She might as well accept it; this was her lot in life. This was where she would be forever. She looked down at the start of a blister on her otherwise tender right hand and she knew there would be more as the summer wore on. Her skin would get brown as an Indian's. Her hands would get a little rougher, carrying the cream cans to town every week, to sell at the creamery for grocery money, and her farm girl shoes, well, they would scuff up. After they saw how harvest went this fall, she would get some new clothes. That is just how things went every year on the farm.

Christopher and Zack did the lion's share of the farm work, and there was no shortage of work to be done on a farm. From sun up to sun down, someone had to gather eggs, feed chickens, and feed out the hay. Never was there a moment they were not hoisting something, it seemed. Those horses and cows always needed to eat. If the cows did not eat well, there would be nothing to sell at the creamery, and then there would be no shoes, no haircuts, and no new coats.

Gertrude did try sewing a couple of winters ago. She made Zack a shirt to go to a school dance with Peggy Warren. It was the brightest shade of purple, and Gertrude had fashioned it from some material she'd found in Mama's sewing basket in the back of a wardrobe. She thought Zack might have appreciated that a little bit. That purple shirt was such a disaster, and persnickety old Peggy Warren was so embarrassed, she never spoke to Zack again. He told his little sister to mind her own business and they would get their shirts in town, thank you very much. Gertrude thought that may not have had so much to do with her sewing skills, as it did a particularly disastrous kissing incident that the whole town knew about and Zack just wouldn't admit.

Gertrude knew there had to be more. There had to be more than just this little town in North Dakota, with its Main Street and its dirt. She wanted to know what else was out there, but she wasn't so sure she wanted to go to the Teacher's School, in order to spend the rest of her life working in a school.

When Mr. Anderson dismissed class, Gertrude gathered her books, lined them up carefully in her knapsack, in A-B-C order, because that is how she liked things, and slung it over her right shoulder. She lifted her lunch pail with her left hand, from the floor where it had been all day, its plain cheese sandwich and apple still tidily tucked inside. She hadn't had much of an appetite lately, and she didn't seem to be hungry, either. Maybe she was depressed, or nervous about her future after graduation. Or maybe she was in love.

A BOY WITH A CAR

Gertrude had walked not even halfway home from school, and she heard the sputter of his Model A. Gertrude knew he was driving up behind her, so she didn't bother to turn around. The car got closer and closer, and finally rolled so close to Gertrude that it nearly ran her off into the wheat field. She resisted the temptation to fire sparks out of her sea-glass green eyes at Billy Ray. Any attention, even feigned annoyance, was good attention, as far as he was concerned, and it only encouraged him.

His mother named him William, for his grandfather, who had fought with the English army. His papa's name was Ray. Everyone called him Billy. Gertie called him Billy Ray when he was in trouble, which, as far as she was concerned, was most of the time.

"Gertie," he hollered. "Get in!"

Gertie immediately did not care for his attempt at getting her attention. That boy would need to be taught some manners.

"Hey, Gertruuuude!"

She would not turn her head. Keep walking, she told herself. He had nearly run her off into the ditch with that—that— machine! And now he was turning her name into some kind of cow call? He would soon learn.

"Gertie, go for a drive with me," Billy Ray pleaded. He was pacing her now, the automobile rolling alongside her as she walked home from school, trying to mind her own business.

"Billy Ray, is that you? I hardly noticed," Gertrude managed, regaining her composure and nicely pulling off a blasé stance, while brushing a curl from her forehead. "If you take me right home, I will get in your car. Otherwise, no. Forget it. I'm thinking about something, and I don't want to be bothered."

"Oh yeah?" Billy Ray asked, trying to catch her eye. Gertrude was gazing at the fields, or the sky. She would look anywhere but at him. "What are you thinking about so intensely that you can't go for a drive with me?" She gave him no answer, for this conversation merited none.

"Well," he started again. "I'm thinking, too," Billy Ray said slowly. "I've been thinking about you all day."

Gertrude stopped walking, and her knapsack slid off her shoulder to the crook of her elbow.

"Is that so?"

Her reddish-brown hair was glimmering in the late afternoon Dakota sun, which caught the golden highlights and gave her a halo.

"I was thinking you were an angel," Billy Ray dripped charm from both corners of his mouth.

The magic complement did the trick. Gertie smiled a half smile, in spite of herself, wondering what on earth this fella was up to. Wasn't he terribly tired, after roofing that old house all day? She climbed into his car. But he didn't take her home, as requested. They drove through the middle of town, down by the river, out by his pop's farm, through the pasture, and past the cows. Billy Ray honked and hollered at the cows, to move them out of their way.

"Dairy Princess comin' through!" Billy Ray yelled, which was barely audible above the cranking of his Model A. "Make way for the Dairy Princess!"

Gertie's eyes narrowed, one eyebrow raised suspiciously and a wry smile played at her lips.

"Princess?" Gertie jabbed Billy Ray in the ribs, and he squirmed away, as far toward his driver's side door as he possibly could while still driving the car with both hands, and operating the clutch. "Why not the queen?" she demanded.

Just as Gertie's stomach was aching from laughter, Billy Ray rolled to a stop. The stars had begun to twinkle, and a faint haze on the northern horizon hinted at an aurora flare. Gertrude had no earthly idea on whose section line they were, for they had driven around the whole county and her eyes had been overflowing with tears of screaming laughter for an hour.

Their laughter slowed to nonexistence when Billy Ray's expression changed. He looked toward Gertie and put his arm along the top of the car seat.

"May I kiss you?" Billy Ray asked her, timidly, carefully playing with a curl on her shoulder, and trailing his fingers down her spine. He leaned toward her.

"No," responded Gertie. "I've got to get home."

Billy Ray nodded and backed away. He drove Gertie home. Still holding her schoolbooks and lunchpail, she reached up to straighten her hair as they approached the house. Gertrude was a little apprehensive that her pop would be up, waiting for her to come home, and sure enough, there he was, rocking slowly back and forth in that old green rocking chair on the front porch, which could really use some paint itself. The Model A rolled to a stop at the picket fence at the end of the walk.

"Well, come on in the house," Pop said, as he stood in the twilight. Gertie and Billy Ray glanced at each other, on her face, a look of utter terror, but his expression was one of calm, cool, collectedness. Billy Ray squeezed Gertie's hand as a means of reassurance, and helped her out of the passenger side of his Model A. Pop observed this, and nodded inwardly.

They walked hand-in-hand along the front path through Gertie's mother's flower garden, which the family tried to keep up every summer as a labor of love and in memoriam, and entered the house.

Pop had the coffee pot on.

"Have a seat," he gestured toward the kitchen table. With one rough, strong farmer's hand, he poured the coffee, and put lunch on the table. There were plates of gingersnap cookies, summer sausage and cheese. He was slicing bread as he was talking.

"Here, Pop," Gertie was already at the counter. "I'll do this. Go ahead and sit down."

"Sit. The boys are in the barn," Pop said, although he didn't have to tell Gertie. She knew where the boys were. It was milking time. The cows had to be milked at the same time every morning and night, or they would put up a fuss. No one wants to mess with a fussy cow. Gertie certainly did not. She sat, obediently, and never taking her eyes off the nervous interaction brewing between her father and her suitor.

"I figured this day was coming," Pop continued. "Gertrude, your face is red. I realize you're not a little girl any longer, but young man, if you're going to be courting my daughter, you will have the decency to come to my front door.

"Yes, sir," Billy Ray said, which was almost a whisper, but he whispered it loudly enough to be respectable, and so that Pop could hear it.

Pop nodded, outwardly this time. Gertie could see a smirk playing at the corners of his mouth, beneath his thick mustache. That would do.

She had to admit, she felt a little powerful at this moment, given that her father approved of Billy Ray, but that he was a bit intimidated by Pop. This could be useful.

Being that it was springtime, it was planting and calving time. Farmers were up all hours of the night, out in the barns, watching the cows, helping to bring new calves into the world, and the boys were not in school, because they were needed in the field.

In the weeks that followed, Gertie and Billie Ray were inseparable. They spent Saturday afternoons, after their respective morning chores, gazing into each other's eyes out at Sweet Briar Dam and feeding the ducks and geese. During one such Saturday afternoon, Billy Ray offered Gertie a canoe ride in his father's old rickety boat that he had tied to the rumble seat, but Gertrude declined. She didn't mean to hurt Billy Ray's feelings, but one glance at that little schooner told her that it wouldn't make it off the dock. She was touched by his romantic gesture, and when he jumped in the water to prove to her the boat was sound, she felt she had no choice but to swim along. So much for the boat.

Gertie almost lost her shoes that day.

Billy Ray drove her home from school every day in that Model A of his, of which he was so proud.

His mama was rather sickly, so Billy Ray couldn't introduce her to Gertie, and Gertie was sure to understand. His father was working himself to death in the field. They had a small farm, and he and his pop were alone to run it. They raised barley, unlike Gertie's pop, who raised wheat and cows, potatoes and corn, along with a few other things, in the garden. Billy Ray's family life seemed somewhat suspect. Gertie didn't ask too many questions, because she didn't like to see him become uncomfortable and she didn't want Billy Ray to get upset. She remembered her own father's words, that everything usually came out in the wash, and it would all work out in time.

Sometimes when she was lying in bed at night, about to drift off to sleep, staring at the shiny white moon out her window, she thought she could actually still hear that car sputtering.

For Gertie and her friends, school days droned on. There were only a few more formalities they had to endure, really. They were practically finished, and then they had to make decisions. Mary knew what her entire life looked like already, down to the color curtains in her kitchen, for they were the yellow curtains her mother was sewing. Spencer, Mary's fiancé was anxiously awaiting Mary's hand in marriage, the day after graduation, so she would join him in the house he had been working in for months already. Mary's mother would likely have the curtains hung next week.

Gertie sighed a little. Oh, if only she knew what tomorrow held, she would not be so concerned with the rest of her life. She was not envious of Mary and Spencer, not at all, but sometimes she thought it would be nice to have an inkling as to her future. Gertie smiled. Maybe she would make her own adventure. On Graduation Sunday, Gertie did not cry. A lump rose in her throat as the small school band played, "Pomp and Circumstance," but Kristina Jackson put up such a fuss, crying and sobbing theatrically, she fell down into a pile of tears, right there in the procession, in the Lutheran Church, and the trumpet player started giggling.

That was that. The whole sanctuary arose in either a gasp or a roar of laughter, as that poor girl had to be helped to her feet by her little brother and her best friend, and neither of them could bear the thought of leaving Durham. The band did not have any idea what to do, whatsoever. They might as well have brought out kazoos, Gertie thought to herself. Gertie did not understand the idea of looking backward, and of not ever wanting to move beyond the present. Didn't the planet earth only move in one direction? Gertrude decided that's why God made the sun rise every morning in the same place. She was aching to see what else the world had to offer, and wondered how she could do that, just what would she do now? She had not decided what her vehicle would be, whether a wagon, a herd of dairy cattle, or that Model A sitting outside the church right now.

When the seniors departed the church after graduation, Papa was standing next to the Model A with Billy Ray. Billy Ray had a bouquet of daisies and black-eyed susans. Gertie thought they looked pretty, and that it was nice. Papa hugged her, kissed her on the forehead and told her he would see them at home later. Her brothers were working in the field.

Billy Ray handed her the flowers with such an uncertain, forced flourish, the lump in Gertie's throat dropped down into her chest and made her heart swell with adoration. This young man - her young man - was very close to perfect, she was sure of it. His eyes, and his honesty had her in their clutches, tighter than he'd held those flowers, and he was now grasping her hand. It was going to be a good summer.

The days flew by in a dusty blur around gravel roads and down section lines. There were lazy Sundays, holding onto fishing lines, and for Gertie, endless gazing into blue eyes and blue skies. She never thought this summer would end.

Nowhere, Everywhere

2

Gertie was stomping away so hard, she could hear her shoes clomping the dry, August Dakota earth. Her face was hot. Her tears were hotter.

"I love you, you know," she'd finally told Billy Ray. They'd driven out to the middle of his daddy's land, in his Model A, and had spent the afternoon on the banks of the Missouri. They fished, had a picnic, and right about now were stargazing. It was a typical, beautiful day. The silence was uncomfortable, and Billy Ray did not once return her gaze as she made this initial admission of adoration to him.

"I don't mind that," he said.

He didn't mind that? Was he serious? Is that what she deserved after holding back that sentiment from him all this time, and then delivering it, like a precious gift, from a pauper, to the prince?

I don't mind that?

Those words were certainly not what she expected, after all they had had quite the romantic summer. He had spoken of a dreamy future, building her a house and they would fill it with children, laughter, friends, holidays. The more she recalled, the more she cried. The more she cried, the harder her heart became, and the hotter her head got. She felt her hair sticking to her forehead, and she knew her face was getting puffy.

She was angry. No, no, not angry. Mad. Upset. Terribly, terribly upset, and she was not going to let him see her cry. She felt like she'd been toppled to the floor, and had been tossed to the furthest corner. She was humiliated. She was not going to let him see these hot tears of rage, or pain, or whatever they were, because he wouldn't *mind* them anyway. After all, she loved him. She'd said so, and he had dismissed her. Carelessly.

Gertie fell into her bed and cried. It all fell out of her, through her tears, her mother's death years ago, her father's not knowing how to raise a girl, her brothers being so absent. They had each other. In their treatment of her, they were mean and nice and not knowing how to react to her. Basically, all of the unknowing was flowing out of her eyes now, in big, wet, dripping teardrops, and soaking her quilt. She couldn't stop. She'd stepped in and been the lady of the house, cooking and cleaning, and because her pop didn't want her to do all of the work, her brothers shared in it, in addition to working the fields and the barn and the cows. Gertie cried. She wanted her mother there with her. She wanted to ask her mother what

Billy Ray meant when he said, "I don't mind."

Honestly, Gertie thought to herself, was that an appropriate way to respond to such an admission of feelings?

"I don't mind that"? Gertie did not think so. That rapscallion. Had Billy Ray said, "I love you," first, she would have been tover the moon, then she would have tried to remain calm, then would have thrown out the notion of remaining calm, decided they should discuss what love meant, after their spring and summer together, and then moved forward.

Gertie glanced at the Vogue fashion magazine on her bedroom floor. Flappers, dripping in satin and pearls, were dancing on the cover as if they had not a care in the world. Gertie picked up the magazine and flipped through a few pages until the words of St. Augustine leapt at her. "The world is a book and those who do not travel read only one page."

Vogue flappers are not dairy princesses, thought Gertie. And that was when it came to her. She was going to move forward now. She was going to move as forward as forward moved, even if she had to go around the world to do it.

That was it. She had to get away from him. She could not let him see her cry. That would be weak. She was not going to let him see her face again or perceive her as being weak, because that just would not do. If Christopher and Zach caught wind of this, they would surely, without a doubt, kill Billy Ray. She didn't want him dead, she just wanted him… sorry. Her tears were lulling her to exhaustion. She would leave this place, without really thinking about how.

Gertie awoke to find her pop sitting next to her on her very pink bed. She wiped her right eye, as he was running his rough, rancher's hand down the left side of her pink face to catch any leftover tears.

"Paris, huh?" Pop said. "What's wrong, Trudy? There you were, mumbling about Paris in your sleep again. I know it's not easy being here, being the "girl" around the farm with us, but we'll do whatever you want, whatever we can. Do you want to go to that girls' college? I'll send you. I want you to be happy, sweet pea, and I can't make you happy here."

TYLER

He was dusty, tanned, and his grin beamed mischief. He was young, and his green eyes were just a little bit older. He'd seen a lot. From his cap to his boots, Tyler Texas looked every inch like Little Boy Trouble Grown Up, but Gertie was drawn to his company. He'd blown into town off of a Great Northern Twelve O'Clock this summer, and had been working at the front counter at Mr. Lucky's store for three months now.

"I'm gonna be a cowboy poet," Tyler announced.

They were enjoying a picnic, perched on a fallen cottonwood tree, overlooking the river valley, hills and fields as far as the eye could see.

"Really?" asked Gertie, who could barely keep from laughing at his serious declaration of poetic intentions. She worked herself into a straight face. "Okay, Mr. Cowboy Poet, spin me a yarn. Or, sing me a song. Or, recite me something famous."

Tyler jumped off the log and stood in front of Gertrude with bravado. He held one arm extended toward her, palm facing toward the sky. His left hand was held dramatically over his heart. Gertie had never seen this side of Tyler. She was curious as to what was about to happen.

"I'm gonna jump me a train and Catch Hell
See places I don't know all too well
Gertie, Gertie, won't you come with me
Let's Catch Hell and ride to the sea."

Gertie laughed at the overdelivery of the impromptu poem.
Upon her reaction, Tyler looked a little hurt, and that's when
she realized he was serious.

"Oh, you... You want to go somewhere?"

He nodded, hopefully.

"You're leaving?" Gertie was coming to understand as quickly
as she possibly could.

"I'm going to the ocean, Gertie," Tyler said, dreamily, as he
gazed with vision into the prairie breeze. "Folks can live on
the beach. Cook their dinner right there, on an open fire. "

He turned his Neglected Cherubic face to her.

"Come along."

Well, Gertie justified in her mind, he is adventurous. He is
poetic and dramatic. He tries hard, and he is her best friend. If
she stayed here, nothing would ever change. If she got on a
train, she would at least see some of the country. She hopped
down from the elm branch, planted her fists squarely on her
hips, and announced, "Tyler Texas, Cowboy Poet, I will Catch
Hell with you."

Tyler laughed, a raucous laugh that caused him to pick Gertie
up and swing her around, which made her laugh out loud.

Even as she celebrated having made a decision to move in a direction, doubt ran through her mind for just one moment, a blink. She would need to tell Pop. She would have to say goodbye to Billy Ray. Before she let herself fully think about approaching Billy Ray with a goodbye, or a hello, or an empty cream can, Gertie remembered that he *wouldn't mind* what she did. She decided he didn't need to know a thing. She would go straight away with Tyler to talk to her father.

To "Catch Hell," in those days was to hop a train without a ticket.
Telling her pop where she was going was somewhat fearsome. He handled it better than she did. With her brothers sitting right there, he gave her a thousand dollars, which Tyler did not see.

Gertie packed Mama's white suitcase, with various things she would want or need, and then began to edit herself. As a young woman, she would not bring her teddy bear, or her favorite bracelets, but she wasn't going anywhere without the family picture from a few years back, before her mother took ill, in that cameo pen pin. It had been hanging on the lamp in her bedroom for months, its silver nearly tarnishing, and the engraved script, "I Love You," greeting her as the sun broke through her window in the mornings. Pop hugged her fiercely, kissed her forehead, and told her that a farm is no place for a girl her age. She should see the world, and she should see it now, while she was young. He wanted her to write, and to write often. Her ancestors had been adventurers, he told her. She should find her Promised Land. He did not cry. But Gertie did. Pop took Gertie by the shoulders, and walked her back out into the front room to the door. He handed her satchel to Tyler and shook his hand fiercely, saying, "Take care of my little girl."

"Yes, sir," said Tyler Texas, in the meekest fashion of anything he'd ever uttered.

As Zach and Christopher hugged their sister goodbye, they tried to hide the dampness in the corners of their eyes. The time for moving on had commenced.

3

It may have been the usual daily bustle and hustle of the depot that Gertie had never noticed before. She felt every eye on her, not necessarily on Tyler, as they prepared to toss their bags into a boxcar and hop the train before it left. Of course no one was inspecting them, Gertrude had a guilty feeling about leaving her hometown this way. From a few cars away, she could see Spencer, Billy Ray's best friend, stacking crates on the platform. Spencer looked up and waved. Gertie waved back out of habit, and then, caught her mistake. Spencer would surely tell Billy Ray he'd seen Gertie with that strange fellow from out of town, and that they'd left on a train. Oh well, thought Gertie. She was sure Billy Ray *wouldn't mind*.

The problem was, Gertie couldn't be waving like a Dairy Princess if she was supposed to be jumping into a boxcar and hiding out. To avoid waving at any other old friends and townspeople, she threw her bag into the doorway of the next car they passed, and leapt the gap.

"Whoa!" exclaimed Tyler. "Nice jump!" He followed suit, and soon, they were amidst a shipment of breadbags and fruit crates, headed somewhere out west. "This was a good choice, Gert," Tyler mused. "We'd have had to come up with something to eat the next few days."

Gertie hadn't even thought of that. What to eat? She would have to plan better for the rest of this adventure. The train began to rumble, and so did that feeling in Gertie's stomach when something big was about to happen. Here goes, she thought.
The sky was gray, Gertie noticed, as she frowned to herself. It was grayer over there, exactly where this train was heading. It was amazing to whirr over the prairie as fast as they were going, faster than any Model A. They must have been going at least fifteen miles per hour. Take that, Billy Ray. Tyler Texas was sleeping, rocked back and forth like a baby in the cradle of this boxcar.

Gertie wanted to watch the scenery. This is what she was here for, why she was born. She wanted to see everything. She had to know what else was out there, beyond the bluffs and the prairie dog cities. And, to tell the truth, it looked like more of the same.

"Why did I bother leaving North Dakota?" she mused, as the train rocked over the tracks, and Tyler Texas, soon-to-be World Famous Cowboy Poet, snored in the corner. How big is the world? How long is this going to take? Gertie, admittedly, to herself, but to no one else, is a little impatient. This Riding Rails Adventure would have been grander, had they bought tickets like civilized people, but Tyler wanted the experience of Catching Hell, the cold of the boxcar, and then he fell into a deep sleep. She should really check to make sure he was still alive. A fine travel partner he turned out to be.

Gertrude shouldn't have done this. She shouldn't have left home, to take off running across the country with this wild, sleepy, boring cowboy dreamer. She felt so lonely, so literally beside herself, and this train just kept rolling. It felt like this would never end. All she could hear was the sound of the train on the railroad tracks, usurped by the snoring next to her. How long could this possibly go on? What happens when they get where they're going? Gertrude thought of the money in her satchel. Her pop had given her a thousand dollars, a whole thousand dollars of the cream money he'd been holding back, even from the bank, and she had hidden it in her train case. Tyler did not need to know everything. A little knowledge could be a dangerous thing. Gertrude could probably get anywhere on her own, once this train stopped. She began to fantasize about that.

Gertie looked off in the distance and saw what looked like piles of snow pushed up on the horizon. As the train got closer, they looked more like clouds on the ground, or, no, those were the Rocky Mountains.

My goodness, she thought. They are Purple Mountain Majesty. So that is what Lewis and Clark sought to conquer in order to find the Northwest Passage. Gertrude was thankful she'd paid attention in Mr. Anderson's history class, for the most part.

The boxcar became chillier. Tyler awoke. He wrapped his arms around her and nuzzled her neck. They smiled together at the romantic scenery that is western Montana, the Rocky

Mountains, and breathed deeply the scent of pine needles. After a few minutes, Tyler grew bored of the beautiful scenery and his eyelids drooped again. He was no doubt dreaming up the poem that would make him famous.

Gertie felt the lump rise in her throat when she saw the mountains rising, and she smelled the snow. She knew it was anticipation she was feeling, or was it fear? She would have loved to talk it over with this cowboy poet, but he was so busy being a distant, introspective artiste, that she did not dare approach him with her trifling thoughts. The only thoughts that were important were his, when he bothered to be awake. Actual tears fell out of Gertrude's eyes, and off of her chin, even though German girls from the center of North Dakota do not often cry. They deal with situations. She thought again about the dairy money hidden in her satchel, and about how she could get where she wanted to go, and still get back home. She thought about Billy Ray.

Tyler spent his waking hours working out poems and shouting them out the side door into the wind, where they got lost, never to be heard by another human ear. However fast this train was going, no one was going to listen to the nonsense that he was hollering, Gertie thought. Tyler believed he was giving his poems as a gift to the universe, and it would richly repay him. She began to grow more skeptical of him with each passing moment.

Gertrude smelled snow, and it smelled delicious to her, being a small town North Dakota girl. She saw snow clinging to the pine trees as the train lumbered past them and wound through the hills, higher and higher.

As they climbed, the air grew thin and cold. The steam engine driving this train sputtered. Gertie noticed snow on the ground now. She thought about the cows. Zack would be keeping them close to home, in the barn, and giving them more hay when this cold gets to North Dakota. Storms always move from Montana over to North Dakota, and then the wind carries them to Minnesota. The cattle had to eat a lot more in the winter, in order to give the same amount of milk. The cold made them burn more calories. Luckily, it had been a good summer for hay, and they had cut the Widow Chrest's hay fields, as well, so they had extra feed in the barn. Had they not cleared those fields, the hay would have rotted all winter and vermin would have taken up residence, causing problems for all the farmers in the area next summer. It had to be harvested, and they were glad to take it. The cows would be fed this winter, which in turn would feed the family. Hopefully, the spring would bring some good calves.

Gertie felt the train car jerk and rock side to side as it abruptly came to a stop. She braced her short fall to the floor of the boxcar with her forearms. Tyler awoke with a start.

"What happened?" he demanded, groggily.

"I don't know," Gertie said, half crying, half screaming. She was scared now.

Outside, people were running, or trudging rather, in the deep snow toward the front of the train. Gertie watched in fearful wonder as the silver dollar-sized snowflakes continued to fall, straight down, like big chunks of lace. They were big, wet, and dangerous. This was not the windy snow she was used to back home in North Dakota. This snow stayed put where it landed, and melted there in the spring. During the winter, it piled up, causing problems for travel, roofs, animals, and people.

Tyler Texas, Cowboy Poet, could not, not be part of the action. With his characteristic bravado, he swung out the door onto the rungs of the ladder and down, falling flat on his back into the snow at the bottom of the train.

"Don't worry, Gert," Tyler called up to her, as he collected himself and brushed the snow off of his chest and thighs. "I'll find out what's going on." As an afterthought, and without looking in Gertie's direction, he hollered, "Be back."

Gertrude rolled her eyes and smirked to herself as Tyler ran-walked through the fluffy, wet snow on his way to the front of the train. He wanted to be at the middle of the situation. He needed to be the center of attention. Maybe he could help, or make someone laugh. A small, guilty part of Gertie's mind let herself think, *Maybe he would put himself in the center of the problem.*

As Tyler ran off through the snow toward the front of the steam engine, Gertrude went through her knapsack. She slowly counted the money given to her by her father, still not believing, while gratefully believing, that he had handed over one thousand dollars for her safe journeys away from home. She reached in and pulled out the cameo pen that was made for her by a jeweler friend of the family. It was rare and beautiful. It was a cameo, and a pen. She could wear it, and write with it. If she opened it up, there was a portrait of her mother on one side, and a portrait of her mother, father, brothers, and herself on the other. On the back, the words, "I love you." Gertrude vowed to herself to keep in touch with her family with this pen.

After what seemed like a long time, Tyler did not return, as he promised he would. Gertie wondered how long it had been, and packed up her belongings once again, slung her knapsack over her shoulder, and leapt to the ground. She followed the tracks already in the snow, until she joined the mobbed crowd at the front of the train, mulling over the busted steam engine.

"What's wrong with it?" Gertie asked a woman on her tiptoes, trying to see past several other shoulders.

"Altitude and weight," the woman said, skeptically. "We're too heavy, and the train is trying to huff and puff over these here mountains. It's broke."

Gertie did not see her cowboy poet anywhere. She thought for certain he would be up on a tree stump, spouting off some limerick about steam or wheels or chugalugging, but he was no where to be seen.

"Have you seen Tyler Texas, the Cowboy Poet?" Gertrude asked a man in a white wool coat and a Greek fisherman's cap standing near the crowd of onlookers, thinking he would certainly recognize to whom she was referring. He stood a step back from the rest of the group, seemingly interested, but somewhat unconcerned with the problem that was certainly affecting the fate of everyone on the train.

"Who?" the man asked.

"He's a poet," Gertrude explained, completely believing in Tyler as she was telling the stranger about him. "He takes regular circumstances and makes poems from them. He would see beauty in this debacle, and come up with poetry that would make you cry, it is so good." "Lady, there was a guy here kind of like that," the man said. "But he was the only one crying. He was blathering on and on, while work was trying to get done. He wouldn't be quiet and get out of the way. Always had to be at the center of things while we were trying to talk about what to do, and how to handle it best, and here comes Mr. Poet, wouldn't ya know. So, he got popped in the nose. He has been hauled off to the hospital at Butte. "

"Oh no!" Gertie cried, feeling somewhat responsible for Tyler, but half relieved, too. "Is he going to be alright? Should I go there?"

"Sweetheart, he's more afraid of the sight of blood than anything," he went on. "If you ask me, he's fine. Let him be there by himself. You want my advice? Get back on the train, in the passenger car this time. Get yourself a real man. One who's not afraid of blood. One who doesn't spout off. One who can buy a train ticket and not leave pretty little you to catch pneumonia in the boxcars. How could he leave you in such danger?"

Gertie nodded once, looked at the ground, and looked away. With her knapsack on her shoulder, she took one step toward the train, then another. But wait a minute. The train was not moving. What now? She decided to chance it. All passengers were outside. Tickets had been collected, and if they were going to get another train, they would just move them all, not ask for new tickets. Right? Right!

Gertie looked for a seat that did not have a piece of paper over it.. The pieces of paper indicated to which city the passengers were heading. Some to Seattle, and some of these seats would be carried all the way to California. Gertie had heard things about California, but she wasn't sure she wanted to go there yet. She chose an empty window seat, because she wanted to see her adventure as it came to her. The conductor came through with announcements, and soon, this railcar was connecting to a brand new train bound for Seattle! Gertie would have to think about how the trains connected and helped each other for a long time.

We all want to go somewhere, she thought. *But we can't always go alone.*

Gertie watched as the snow-covered mountain range disappeared into the dusky horizon. She wondered where Tyler ended up, but not for long. This new adventure was too precious, too bold and daring, to be encumbered with old nonsense.

4

The gentleman seated across from Gertie was a dapper man about ten years her senior. He was dressed in a white suit and charcoal overcoat, and was obviously a lawyer or a businessman. He had certainly gone to college, and had not toiled on a farm all his days. He was watching Gertie as she stared out the window, lost in her thoughts, and when she noticed his gaze, she looked at the floor and managed a smile. He spoke.

"The salmon or the sea?" her seatmate asked her.

"Hmm? Pardon me?" Gertie was surprised by such a question.

"Many people go to Seattle for the salmon," said Blair Corey. "Most go for the sea."

"Oh," Gertie understood now. "I'm going… for lack of previous train."

He chuckled at her.

"So you're one of our guests from the steam engine," Blair surmised. "The conductor made that announcement when we stopped at Whitefish. You didn't get hurt, did you?"

Gertie was touched that someone finally asked her how she was doing. After days away from home, this stranger was the first person to look her in the eye and speak directly to her about herself.

"No, no, I'm alright," she managed. "I was travelling with a friend. He was taken to a hospital they said, and I don't know where they've taken him. I guess I'm on this trip alone now. But that's alright, because I am going to see whatever I want to. I am going to see everything."

"Your friend?" Blair asked. "Hospital? There is no hospital for a hundred miles. There would be no way to get him to the hospital down that snowy pass, especially when a train is stuck. Did you see who took him?"

"No," Gertie admitted. "I was writing letters home to my family when he left me in the boxcar to see what why the engine had stopped. But a man… a man in a white coat told me that Tyler had gotten into a fight, so someone hit him. He fainted, and was rushed off down the mountain. They would not tell me where he was."

"White coat, you say?" Blair looked very interested now, and tugged on his overcoat. "Gertrude, that sounds like it may have been more than a punch. I don't want to alarm you, but there is a band of criminals that patrol troublesome mountain passes, and wear white coats. They tend to rob, and sometimes kill. I don't know where your friend is. Be careful whom you trust, my dear."

"Oh. Oh no!" Gertie began to cry. Blair moved over to sit next to her and put his arms around her.

"There, there, my dear," he cooed. "It's going to be okay now. We'll get you to Seattle and you'll have your adventure. Show me a smile."

Gertie found Mr. Corey to be somewhat instantly familiar, but extremely kind. She was surprised by how relaxed she was with this man in the white suit.

Blair wiped her tears away with the kerchief from his vest pocket, and Gertie did her best to smile. To think, Tyler Texas, Cowboy Poet, could have been murdered! Indeed, her friendship with Tyler, the center of attention, had taken a strange turn since boarding the train. He seemed to lose the exuberance he had back home. She never felt good enough, because he put down all of her thoughts as uninteresting, not funny, not artistic enough, not eloquent enough, not poetic enough and then he would turn around and say the same thing she had just said and make it rhyme, and suddenly, he was brilliant, in his own mind. He had told her he loved her that day, back home, and once she hopped on the train, he never again told her she was pretty, or that he was glad she was there. It hurt. It made her want to turn the train around. Gertie wanted to do the impossible, because of the impossible Cowboy Poet.

Looking out the window, Gertie marveled at the beauty and

bigness of the mountains. There were so many trees, and trees just did not grow like this back in   North Dakota. When the train had chugged down its final mountain pass, Gertie turned to Blair Corey, who was reading newspapers and making notations on documents from his satchel, and he looked up and smiled kindly at her.

"It's close now," he calmly told her. "The ocean is coming to you."

As if it was rising up out of nowhere, the mountain range faded away behind the train, and a big, blue horizon loomed out before Gertie. She could not believe her eyes. The Rocky Mountains with their snow caps had been one thing, and she had seen snow before. She had never expected this. This was the Pacific Ocean. Gertie had the sensation that she was standing on a globe in a classroom back in elementary school, and someone gave it a good spin. It was dizzying, for a landlocked girl to be introduced to this much water.

The train turned, and luckily enough, Gertie's window was oceanside, so she could view the blue immensity all the way into the station.

Here was the station, Gertie began to think to herself. She jumped on a train as a vagabond back home in North Dakota. She was detraining in a rather classy fashion in Seattle, Washington, with a dapper gentleman.

"Congratulations on your graduation," Mr. Corey began. "Perhaps you will consider what kind of work you will pursue. If you do not wish to become a teacher, there are opportunities with my organization. These are discussions we will have."

"First thing's first," Blair announced, as he took her by the hand and helped her down from the train step. "Let us go get you a dress for dinner."

Mr. Corey hired a carriage, and helped Gertrude up the step. She was used to riding in wagons back home to get some of the fieldwork done when the machinery was out of commission, but this "wagon" seemed so fancy! It was white, and had curlicues on each side, with red velvet seats. Gertie felt like the Queen of England, or one of Santa's elves, she couldn't decide for certain which one. Blair said something to the driver that she could not hear, and he sat back and put his arm around her. His smile and his reassuring arm gave her a sense of safety. She finally felt she could relax a little. Here was a man who would handle things. Here was a man with whom she did not have to feign interest, for Blair Corey was so very interesting.

The carriage came to a halt. Blair helped her down and thanked the driver. He guided Gertie inside a dress shop with so many beautiful frocks on the walls and every which way, that Gertie became self-conscious of her current garment. She'd been on the train for days, let alone in her farm girl traveling clothes.

"Mr. Corey!" exclaimed a brightly painted face from among the mannequins, as she bobbed forward. "How lovely to see you!"

"Angelica," Blair began. "This is Gertie. We are traveling. She needs some things. I knew you could help us."

"Why, you've come to the right place, you know," Angelica's golden head nodded. "Where are you off to now?"

"Japan," Blair informed her. "We'll need everything."

Gertie's eyes widened. She thought she was only picking out a dress for dinner. She turned her head toward Blair and blinked. He chuckled when he saw her face.

"You did want an adventure, Miss Gertrude," he said. "Would you like to cross the ocean, see the dolphins, experience the Orient? I will take you. We will be working there."

Gertie felt the breath go out of her. She nodded, because all of that sounded wonderful, and like something she would never have done otherwise. She would cross the ocean with this man. That big, big blue entity she saw coming into Seattle today? She would conquer it. Take that, Billy Ray. Take *that*.

Angelica dressed Gertie up and dressed her down. As Gertie tried on dresses, feeling like a doll, she looked for an indication of price, knowing she had her own budget to keep, and Angelica waved away her worries.

"You won't have to worry about a thing," Angelica assured Gertie. This thought was seeded deep in Gertrude's mind as perhaps a bit suspicious, but Blair had mentioned a trip, and perhaps a job in the future with his company? And he was such a nice man! Alone in the world outside North Dakota, Gertie decided to be thankful.

Blair sat in a chair at the front of the shoppe and read a Seattle newspaper, while going through the papers in his satchel again. He would give his approval on this dress or that one, or he liked red better than blue.

Angelica added some eye makeup and a deep red lipstick to

Gertie's face. Gertie had never been made up before. She felt very glamorous.

Dressed in a deep green cocktail dress with matching shoes and a pashmina, her hair swept into a chignon, Gertrude stepped back from the mirror to meet herself for what felt like the first time. She barely recognized whom she saw.

Angelica spoke with a lilt in her voice.

"What a transformation, my dear pet," she said. "You are such a beautiful woman."

Angelica held up the small makeup bag and gestured to Gertrude that it would be in a smaller shopping bag, so she would be able to find it again easily.

As Gertie walked across the boutique toward Blair, she heard each of her steps echo in her mind. It was dark outside, and the only light on the street was from a few gaslights coming in through the windows. She had no idea how many hours she had been there, trying on clothes like a dress up doll, but she certainly had had a lot of fun. Blair never took his eyes off of her as she approached him. He stood up.

"Angelica," he began, looking dead-on at Gertie. "She is stunning. "We will need a steamer trunk."

"I have already got it packed and it is ready to go, Mr. Corey," Angelica assured him. "You said you were going to Japan, so I didn't think you were going to carry her things out of here today." She smiled so brightly. Gertie thought the sun had come out again. She would very much like to be friends with someone like Angelica.

Blair went to the counter and signed a piece of paper. Then he came back to Gertie and took her by the hand.

"Darling," he said. "May I take you out on the town?"

"Darling?" Gertrude thought. *Well, I never!*

In a green cocktail dress, with a green feather in her green cap, and green sparkles on her green shoes, Gertie was treated like a lady on the town that night, not a girl from the farm. She was dined at an elegant hotel, she was whirled around the dance floor during every dance. Gertie very nearly forgot her that in her suitcase, not so far away, rode her scuffed, brown, barn shoes. She felt very glamorous tonight.

What a nice man, Gertie thought. Blair made arrangements for her hotel and told her they would be sailing very early.

Sailing, Gertie mused. Wait. *Sailing? In a boat?*

There would be no sleeping. Gertie, a young lady of landlocked origin, could think of nothing else but all of that water beneath her feet. What then?

The Challenge was the name of the Ocean liner that would carry them to the Orient. It was monstrous. Gertie had never seen anything like this. The activity aboard *The Challenge* was not unlike that of an anthill, and she found it a bit humorous and a little disturbing that there were going to be so many people and things aboard this ship. Would it not sink from sheer weight? No matter, thought Gertie, she was with Blair, and if she died with Blair, all would be right with the world.

Gertie took in the bustling scene at the dock, which had nearly overwhelmed her, and thought of Billy Ray's broken-down canoe in the pond back home, the afternoon last summer when they both ended up swimming with their picnic basket. This was a big, strong ship. It would be alright.

She would have to devise a plan in which Blair would eventually meet her family but never, ever see her home. She had no idea how she was going to do that. At her core, she felt a little guilty, thinking about hiding her pop and brothers, and their proud, hardworking ways. A tiny smile turned up the sides of her lips as she thought of her mother's flower garden out in front of the house, beyond the porch, that her father had been keeping up so carefully, as a labor of love for his late wife all of these years. But she just could not imagine the fancy Blair Corey ever coming to visit her in North Dakota.

Being at sea was a trifle unsettling for a Midwestern girl like Gertie, who had grown up in the wide open country of North Dakota, never having seen the beach, except at the lake. At the lake, she could see the other side. She was not accustomed to being surrounded on all sides by a tremendous blue, feeling swallowed up by it.

Blair wanted to make Gertie comfortable while sailing, so they went for walks along the seaboard, her arm resting in the crook of his elbow, gazing at the stars, and chatting. The motion of the sea was somewhat similar to the rocking of the train, and Gertie felt for a while like she may never stand solidly again. Perhaps the whole world is in a gentle rocking motion, she mused.

They were best friends, or so she believed. When she would talk, he would look at her and smile, and hum softly. Sometimes, he nodded. Blair rarely engaged in conversation, but he let Gertie talk all she wanted to. What else was there to do on the open sea? Gertie was not sure what his humming and silence meant, but being that she was the only other person in the conversation, she supposed that was alright. She figured he was paying attention, because he was responding in some way. Blair was going to Japan on business, and he had been there before.

Blair asked Gertie if she was interested in becoming his personal secretary. She indeed was intrigued by such work, and would learn what he needed and wanted. Blair told her she would come to know in time. She did not have to worry about such matters now. She did not know just what that meant, but she became very comfortable with Blair. She waited for him to give her work assignments, but it appeared he just wanted her to travel with him. He assured Gertie she would find the Japanese culture to be colorful, the food to be interesting, and this adventure would be one she would remember for the rest of her life.

Gertie's conversations with Blair were nothing like her talks with Tyler, or her long-winded laughing and soul-baring sessions with ol' Billy Ray back home. Billy Ray… Gertie wondered what Billy Ray was doing right now. It had been three months since she had seen him, since he had broken her heart in that field. She had told him she loved him, and he told her he didn't mind that.

What could happen in six months? For all she knew, he was married by now, working his pa's barley fields with a baby on the way. Who was she to even think about him? The Dairy Princess two-years-in-a-row, that's who! She would show Billy Ray! She would send him a postcard from the other side of the world! She wondered if he would *mind that.*

After many days, land was visible on the blue horizon. Gertie was relieved at the thought of standing on dry ground again, and began to breathe deeply, tinged with sadness. Her runaway adventure with Blair Corey was coming to an end, and entering a new stage. What would they do in Japan? Where would they go?

5

Japan was, in a word, dizzying. It was loud. It was busy. There were more people here than any place Gertie had ever been. The colors were brighter than Gertie had ever seen. This environment terrified her and thrilled her. How long would they stay? She asked Blair when they got to their hotel, a confusing little hut with dark, almost black, wood walls, a few rooms, and rich red brocade fabrics, unlike anything Gertie had ever seen. He smiled at her in that quiet way, which told her he wasn't going to tell her. He was going to be in control.

Blair made it clear that he had meetings and work to do all of the time, it seemed, and he was still very kind to Gertie. He explained that he did not have the time for her that he had while they were traveling on the ship. Blair told Gertie it was not necessary that she, as his personal secretary, attend meetings with him. This surprised Gertie, but she was not going to feel abandoned. After all, she had gotten further on her adventure than she ever thought she would.

Gertie set about the business of seeing the sights of Japan on her own. She was determined to see every inch of Osaka, touch all of its fabrics, and taste all of its food. She spent her days wandering the streets of this city, which was completely on the opposite side of the world from her wheat fields and Pa.

Gertie stood on the pier late one morning, gazing out at the sea. She was on the other side of the planet from Billy Ray. She had travelled so far away, she did not think she could have been further from him, yet, with one warm little feeling inside her ribs, it was as if he may have followed her to the end of the universe, and he could tiptoe up behind her at any time. Gertie realized she was smiling in spite of herself, and her eyes were closed. She shook herself out of her reverie.

A thought of love of another is a prayer, Mama had told her, long years ago, before she became so very weak, so very ill, and died. So she didn't feel like she was being dishonest to Blair by praying for Billy Ray. Although, she certainly wasn't going to tell Blair about it.

Blair's work kept him very occupied. As the weeks wore on, his mind began to be far away, and conversation with Gertie lulled. He rarely smiled at her anymore, and though their conversations had often been rather one-sided on Gertie's part, he now was not involved at all. She wondered why this kind, wonderful man had suddenly fallen away from their closeness? She went so far as so ask him about it one evening as they shared dinner and sake.

Blair said nothing. Gertie pressed on, asking for an answer.

Wordless, he leaned back and stood up from the floor cushion, and walked toward the door.

"Blair?" Gertie began, as she stood to follow him toward the door.

"Nein! Sietz diech!" he snarled, whipping around to face her, and in doing so, catching Gertie's cheekbone with his hand. "No! Sit down! Be quiet!"

Mumbling something about his meeting, Blair donned his hat and overcoat, picked up his satchel and left, rather in a huff.

Gertie froze and she felt a trembling in her chest. She could not believe what had just happened. She replayed the previous moments in her mind several times, as she felt the hot spot on her face. The air closed in around her, and she formulated a plan. She was unaware Blair could speak any German at all. If he was so easily angered, and would use such a tone with her, she would not stay and hear it, or wait for the danger that was coming.

Before things spun further out of control, Gertie took the situation by the reins and began to formulate a plan. She knew the continent was further west, thanks to the maps on the walls of the teahouse in the city, and she knew the boats left at dawn. She had been on the pier to watch them. Gertie sprung to action.

Gertie searched the drawers of Blair's wardrobe, finding large bills. *Ten thousand dollars!* Why did he have all of this money here, and not in a bank? Upon further rifling, Gertie found papers written in German and Japanese. She knew Blair had business in Japan, and this confused her. He did not speak about his business, and she did not ask. There were several numbers – they looked like combinations of locks – covering pages and pages of paper. After living in Japan for several months, Gertie could make out only the heading on the page, but the German translation was clear as day:

Kommunistische.

Blair was a Communist? What *is* a Communist, exactly? Gertie realized she had not taken a breath in several seconds. She remembered the wisdom of Pa's words: "Beware of any man too involved in causes, Gertie. If something doesn't seem quite right, it probably isn't."

"The Lord, The Land, and The Family," were Pa's causes. He didn't have to hide them in drawers or hold secret meetings at night. Blair Corey was a man undeserving of being in her Pa's family, as far as Gertie was concerned, and she did not want to be here when he returned.

Gertie packed tightly her dear things into her suitcase-- the pin with the miniature family portrait from so long ago, before Mama fell ill, and some papers. She packed some clothes. A girl needs certain things.

It was already late, and a storm was brewing. Her overcoat was by the door, next to the umbrella stand. Mai, the owner of the tea house, greeted Gertie at the door and welcomed her inside. They were good friends after these months, and Gertie knew she could trust Mai.

Not having ever come to the teahouse, Blair would never know where Gertie's first stop had been. Not having any real interest in agriculture, the businessman Blair would not have cared about the comings and goings of the fishing and rice boats at sunrise. A farmer's daughter from the middle of North Dakota knows to whom she can turn when the storm rolls in.

Over strong green tea, the plan was hatched. Mai would open the teahouse as usual in the morning. At dawn, Mai's husband, Lee, would accompany Gertie to the dock to board Uncle Dayo's rice boat. Uncle Dayo lived with Mai and Lee. Uncle Dayo was the brother of Mai's mother. He was a good man, willing to help where he could, and had a heart for his sister's children. Uncle Dayo had spent his years sailing, and never married or had children of his own. He carried rice to the outlying islands, and Gertie could travel as far west as she wanted. In time, he would return to her location and continue to bring rice and tea.

Gertie rested on a mat in Mai's tearoom that night, breathing in the smells of drying teas. She wondered if she was doing the right thing, fleeing from Blair. He had been kind to her in the past. He had offered her employment with his "organization," but he never did tell her what organization she would be working for. When she saw his face change and found the evidence of Blair's working with the German government and the Japanese government, against the Americans, Gertie knew she had to be as far away from him as possible. In fact, she may want to be safely back home, away from the sea, on the farm, feeding cows and threshing hay. Gertie wondered how long it would take to get there. In the darkness, with her eyes closed, Gertie shook her head and asked for forgiveness. She felt like she had betrayed her country.

At daybreak, the fire was lit to heat the water for tea. Mai embraced Gertie with tears in her eyes. She gave her friend packages of tea for the journey.

"Thank you for English," Mai stammered, trying very

courageously to keep from crying. Gertie smiled. Perhaps she had selfishly been teaching Mai English, so she had someone she could talk to. They agreed she must be on her way, for the boats cannot wait. Lee carried Gertie's bags, which now included things from Mai.

"That's convenient," pondered Gertie, who was a pretty self-sufficient young lady, but she missed having her brothers around to do her heavy lifting.

The dock was not far from the teahouse. Uncle Dayo stood at his vessel, watching expectantly, and perhaps a little impatiently, for this extra passenger. He had risen in the night, to arrive at his boat and prepare for travel. He did not like being put off schedule.

6

As the rice boat left the dock and embarked on its journey, Gertie felt a bit of fear in the pit of her stomach, much akin to that time the bull got loose in the pasture, and Zach and Christopher thought they should be Spanish bullfighters, with Mama's Christmas tablecloth. Oh, she had been so indignant with her brothers! For one, that was a precious memory of their mother, and for two, why was it always on her shoulders to keep her brothers from getting themselves killed?

On the open sea again, standing on the deck of the rice boat, Gertie felt the wind in her hair. Oh, she loved the wind! This was so different than the ocean liner, *The Challenge*!

Uncle Dayo was a big, strong, fatherly man. His skin was a little darker than most Japanese, from being in the sun on the sea all of his days. He reminded Gertie quite a lot of Pa. He was a rice trader, but he also did some fishing, after the boat was empty of rice. There was, not surprisingly, very little conversation between the two, and Gertie watched as the man skillfully adjusted the sails.

Gertie really had not thought about where she would like to go, and until this point, had taken this adventure as it came to her. Here and now, out in the middle of open water, on a boat that felt very small, Gertrude began to panic. She closed her eyes and tried to calm herself, thinking of Billy Ray's broken up canoe, which was the wrong memory to call to the forefront of her mind at this time. A splintered, sunken watercraft was no comfort at all.

"Where are we going?" Gertie asked.

Dayo sensed her distress. "You will be happy there," he smiled. "It is a nice place."

And that assurance dissipated Gertie's minor anxiety. She only needed someone to tell her it would all be okay, that now, here, across the world from her family, things were still in control.

Gertie leaned back on the deck and looked up at the stars. The sky looked very much like her own sky, above her own fields in North Dakota. The Northern Star would always lead her home, and Orion, the Hunter, made her feel safe, as if he was watching out for her. It was there, that she knew Mama was safe and well and happy again, and that if Mama was alright, if God could take care of her mother, then she herself would be okay, whatever the road ahead may bring. Her mama had told Gertie of her Grandpa John's seafaring ways, back in the days before North Dakota came to be. Gertie loved being on the ocean. Just think, Mama had said, Grandpa John sailed around the world. Gertie smiled at the stars with tears in her eyes. Just think, Mama. I'm sailing around the world now.

After a few days, and stops on some very small islands to provide rice to villagers, Dayo told Gertie to get up, home is coming. Gertie cried out with joy as she saw land approaching. It looked like an island, but was larger than any they had seen in a while.

"Palau," Dayo said, his accent thick.

Dayo moored the boat and villagers and children ran to them. They seemed to know Dayo, and were elated at his return. Dayo reached into a cloth bag and threw pieces of Japanese candy to the waiting young ones below. After swinging a leg over the deck and climbing down the rough-hewn ladder, he picked up one small boy and raised him to the sky.

Gertie was still descending the ladder, muttering just a little bit to herself that she was rusty at climbing ladders, not having been up in the hay loft back home on the farm lately. She changed her expression quickly when she saw all the small faces, who were curious about her. *Who was this with Uncle Dayo?*

A tall man resembling Uncle Dayo had gathered a circle of islanders, and all seemed intrigued in this newcomer, but pleasant. Dayo introduced the tall man as Datun, his cousin. "Papa Datun," as he was called, was the elder of the community. Dayo began to address the gathered circle. He explained that this was Gertie, and she would be staying with them for a while. Dayo motioned to an older Palauan woman, Melana, who came nearer to him. He put his arm around her shoulders as he said, in a kind voice, that Gertrude would be the, "English teacher." The woman seemed to be pleased.

The island men prepared a fire and a feast was made for Uncle Dayo and Gertie.

"What a paradise," Gertie told Dayo. "Everyone here is so happy."

"Happiness is here," Uncle Dayo agreed, after he placed another bag of rice in the food house.

Palau, being a matrilineal island, is very friendly to women, so Gertie had no fear for her life nor body while there. She thought for a while she could stay on Palau. Palau was under German control, several generations before. She picked up early on, that the language was like nothing she had ever heard. It seemed to be a mix of German, Polynesian, and Japanese.

Gertie knew English and she knew German. She could even speak conversational Japanese, thanks to Mai at the teahouse. Some of the older people on the island spoke a little German, no doubt handed down from the older days of the little isle's history, during the war. Gertie would teach the children a unified English. She had the foresight that Americans would be through here eventually, and when they did come, these children would need to be able to speak to them.

In the beginning, Gertie kept English lessons very simple, but she wanted the children on the island to at least be able to speak to each other, and she wanted to be able to speak to them, if she decided to stay here. It was very beautiful. There didn't seem to be any concept of time on the island. The sun rose, and the sun set, its rose and orange hues reminding Gertrude nightly that she was in paradise.

On the island, Gertie learned more than she thought she would ever know. She learned how to fish, straight from the ocean, with a spear. She became quite good at it. Often, she would fish with the teenagers, as she was only a little older than they. She gardened with the women, and gained particular joy from it, because it reminded her of being back home on the farm, yet none of the fruits or vegetables they grew in the community garden were like Pa's garden back home in North Dakota. These were island plants. The flowers were much more vibrant than any she'd ever seen. She so longed to share these with her father, who was keeping that fenced-in garden alive in front of the house, along the porch, as a loving tribute to her mother. Here, there were no fences, and no looming winter, Gertrude thought. Here, there was no need to store up one's crops. That was why the island people did not concern themselves with time.

Just as Gertie was settling into island living, and the children were making progress with their lessons, she learned that there indeed was a change in the seasons here. The sky grew dark. Someone shouted, and pointed to a rolling darkness on the horizon. Suddenly, the melee was confusing to Gertie. No one on the island had ever put up this much of a fuss about anything before. Men and women were gathering the children and elderly and running toward the trees.

Gertie ran along behind, helping to usher the young islanders, whose legs were not long enough or fast enough to keep up with the crowds. As the community moved en masse, the rain began to fall, causing a panic. It fell lightly at first, cool droplets meant to calm the skin's sweat from running, climbing, and dodging trees and rocks. Midway up the mountain, the sky cracked thunderously and large, angry drops assaulted the islanders. The people frantically climbed higher, until they reached a rock formation Gertie had never seen before in her months on the island, and as she looked around, she saw that the people from the other beach had joined them at the top.

Papa Datun was standing near the top of the rock. He could see what was happening down the beach, and he was observing the winds coming in. All could hear the wind, but here, at the top of this hill, in the curvature of the rock, they were safe from a few dangerous things. Torches were lit to preserve the light as the clouds grew darker. This was their safe place.

Papa Datun looked down at the huts blown in, at all the hard work of the people, being decimated by this storm. He gazed across the hopeful crowd, huddled with their young children, and Gertie, who was very new to the island way of life. He knew they all looked to him for guidance, and Papa Datun looked up toward Heaven, at the black clouds giving abundant raindrops, and laughed. It was a big, hearty, powerful laugh. It was a laugh that echoed in the crevices of rock on the top of the island, and all who could see Papa Datun heard his laughter. They began to laugh with him, for surely if Papa Datun is laughing, we are alright. If Papa Datun is laughing, God will sustain us.

Quite pleased with this agreement, Papa Datun nodded. With raindrops streaking down his own face, he reached his arms out, as if to embrace the population, and what happened next, Gertie would not have believed it, had she not seen it with her own eyes, and heard it with her own ears. The man, through those impossible raindrops, in this cavern, began to sing. It was only one note, or one word at first, but then Melana stepped out of the crowd and added her voice to Datun's. It was some kind of hymn. It sounded joyful. The harmony was beautiful. Her son, Ama joined his mother. One by one, and two by two, the islanders forgot they were in a storm and took off in a joyful round of song. It was dizzying.

Sometimes, Gertie thought, as she smiled at the unfolding miracle, what we need is someone to teach us to laugh in the darkness, and sing in the storms. What looked like hundreds of people, maybe thousands, were now singing. Gertie could not have counted them all. She had not known these people were all on the island. The songs became louder, and the islanders were more joyful in their singing, defiantly proclaiming victory over this tempestuous interruption of their beautiful life. In none of her travels, since leaving North Dakota, and her grandmother's piano, had Gertie so profoundly felt God in church, than in the middle of a hurricane, at the top of an island bursting with praise.

7

As near as Gertie could estimate, it must be about November. Time did not seem to pass on the island, and children aged by growing up, or taller. Gertie knew that for herself, she would have a birthday soon. Celebrations, dancing, and singing were quite common on the beach, and Gertie assumed that birthdays were somehow being observed.

Uncle Dayo had not returned for some time. Gertie had expected him to come again, but after the day he brought her to this island on his rice boat, he had sailed away. Uncle Dayo was not a young man, Gertie told herself. Neither was he an inexperienced sailor. Storms, like the one she had recently witnessed, were probably not new to Uncle Dayo. Throughout her travels, Gertie had learned that people who come into your life can quickly disappear. She was thankful for her old friend Tyler Texas and Uncle Dayo, and their part in her journey.

Sometimes, during school on the beach, while the Palauans were sitting in the sand and Gertie was pacing back and forth in front of them, speaking to them first in German and then repeating the words in English, the group would catch a glimpse of a far-off ship on the horizon. The first time this happened, Gertie began to yell.

"Over here!" she cried, at the top of her lungs. "We're here! Please! Come help!" Gertie waved her arms and ran along the beach, with five or six Palauan boys and girls chasing her, thinking this was a game they were playing.

"Here! I'm here!" Gertie collapsed in a heap onto the sand, crying and gasping, realizing this tactic was hopeless, and missing her father and the farm, and her mischievous brothers, and those crazy cows that she did not think she would ever miss again. She was worried about her pop.

For the first time since leaving North Dakota with Tyler, and then falling in love with romantic Blair, and then leaving him, because his temperament had changed so, and it frightened her, striking out on her own, and landing on this island, Gertie was admitting to herself that she was homesick. She was on the other side of the world from home, felt she would never get back to the fields and the winds of familiarity. Gertie looked around, through her tear-swollen eyes with a new view of the island and saw something new. What she normally perceived as paradise, now seemed to be too empty, without buildings or farms. There really was not much here. Storms ravaged the island - not often - but when a typhoon came through, it seemed like the end of the world.

She may never see her father's face again. Right now, she was desperately heartsick for him, and for home. She began to feel very claustrophobic in the open island air. Gertie looked around herself. The islanders were staring at her, expectantly. She did have somewhat of a position of authority here on Palau. After all, by teaching them English, she was uniting them in language, and she was helping them to better communicate with one another, and bridge the gap between generations. The temptation was strong for Gertie to be okay with the emotions she was feeling, the longing for home, and the desire to dissolve into a pool of tears. But she had people depending on her. There was no time for that now. Gertie admired the islanders, a sweet people, set in their ways of "making do" with what they had, but time and time again winds and waves ripped their world apart. Thinking deeper, Gertie decided Palauans were not so different from North Dakotans. How many times did her pa tell her they would have to "make do" until harvest, or to get through the winter? Gertie decided all people are basically the same. They make do, in order to get their families through the hard season.

Gertie conferred with the Council of the Grandparents. When she told them she loved the island life, they were very pleased, because it had been an honor to host her. She asked for their help in moving on. This was surprising, in that no one had ever left the island, for it was such a beautiful place. Papa Datun nodded.

"Gertrude misses her family," he said. "No one must convince her to stay. Family is a gift from the Heavens, and we must help in her journey."

It was decided that a beach fire would be kept hot and burning eternally, for the purpose of attracting one of the ships. Gertie talked long with the grandparents, to assure them that sailors would likely not do them any harm, as Palau offered no militaristic threat or materialistic booty, and they probably had nothing to fear by inviting a ship to the shore. Some of the grandparents were young when the Germans first sailed through, but an island like theirs posed no threat.

They believed her. The fire was constructed densely, so that it would burn on and on.

On the first day, not enough smoke seemed to emanate from the fire, as the ship continued on its course without so much as one honk from its horn.

Day two. A boat was spotted by one of the older boys, but it gave no sign of acknowledgement of the fire on the island.

This went on for three days. On day three, Gertie and her school of English-learning students were on the beach, learning verb tense, and her back was turned to the sea when the low, faint whistle of the *Averoff* snapped her straight. Her students jumped up from where they sat. Ama, the oldest boy, took off running first. The others followed, and Eliana, who was the littlest, chased after them. It seemed the children thought this was a game. They were trying to catch a ship.

The vessel seemed to float closer, and Gertie could see the blue-and-white Greek jack emblazoned on its bulwark. This was no sailboat. It was a big, blue, steel ship, the color of a storm cloud. There were attachments on her upper decks that the islanders had never seen. Gertie's eyes widened, and she dug her toe slightly into the sand, as she thought for a moment that she hoped these sailors were kind and had a working understanding of English.

Gertie's next, and more urgent, thought, was how fast the ship was moving. The island had no dock. She sent Ama to run quickly and alert the rest of the village to join her down beach, several yards away from where the ship appeared to be approaching. Gertie did not know how fast, or how severe, the impact would be with the beach. Soon, the ship met with the sand. They sailed in quietly, almost poetically, and perhaps almost silently, the ship ceased.

To herself again, Gertie thought that the Greeks know how to maneuver and stop a ship. She wondered how they managed that.

Like bees from a hive, sailors appeared from all doors, windows, and crevices and secured brails and cables on the ground, in the sand, around trees on the island. The anchor was dropped on the beach. The children looked on, hungrily, to run and inspect this wonder occurring in front of their eyes, but none of the grown-ups would allow them to interfere with the process that was underway. Soon, it appeared they were finished. Gertie swallowed, smoothed her hair and her skirt, and stepped forward.

"Hello," Gertie began slowly. "Welcome to Palau."

8

The men were a bit off-guard and did not take it in stride. They looked at each other, mumbled something in Greek, shrugged, called to the rear of the detachment, when another sailor stepped forward. This one was also tanned, black-haired, and blue-eyed.

"Hello," the sailor offered as he walked forward.

Gertie's eyes widened, and she very nearly took two steps backward. His accent was perfect.

"It's alright," he said. "I'm American. This ship found me on Crete, and I've been with them ever since. I'm working to get home."

He extended his hand.

"Chester Tucker," he said. Gertie placed her hand in his and he shook it. It was nice to have an American friend. It had been a long time.

"Where are you from?" he asked.

Gertie chuckled, in a singular, muted way that made her blink and look at the ground momentarily. She pondered the sand for a moment, taking in its innocent wheat-colored naivety, and then her eyes rebounded to the sky, where not a cloud had polluted the azure shield for weeks.

"Nowhere," she smiled. On second thought, smiling brighter, "Everywhere."

Gertie found that she liked this blue-eyed, black-haired American sailor. How did he sail in out of nowhere, just when she needed him? Well, she did not know. She reminded herself that they were in the presence of other people, and she could not jump up and down at the prospect of being rescued, as much as she may have wished to do so. She regained her composure and offered the sailors a tour around the island. They meandered around the huts, along the roads, up to the church rock, where many of the Greek Orthodox sailors crossed themselves and offered prayers. While Gertie described the tour in English, Chester translated in Greek.

Interesting, thought Gertie. And *fun*.

The island children ran and skipped alongside the group of sailors, happy and excited to have this anomaly, this out-of-the-ordinary crew visiting them. Gertrude thought today felt like Christmas, when the family would gather, and everyone was happy and would laugh and play, so pleased were they to be together. As the group neared the beach, Gertie could see that there was something happening. Some of the island men were preparing a fire for a pig roast. The arrival of the ship had thrown the island into a veritable uproar, and the villagers ran this way and that. The women had the trimmings going for a feast, and the scents wafting up from downbeach were enough to make a stomach rumble.

Plum wine flowed, and torches were lit. Hues of pink and orange overtook the azure sky, and stars began to twinkle above as the sun blazed its way into the sea. A few of the older boys took up their instruments on the edge of the gluttonous crowd, and began to create even more of an atmosphere. Gertie took in the entire scene, wishing she could preserve this very moment forever. All of the children were dancing, and many of the older Palauans took to the dance floor.

Gertie began to wonder about Billy Ray as she watched the dancing. She wondered about his shoulders, how muscular they were when doing the heavy lifting on his father's farm. She wondered about his eyes, which were as blue as a Dakota sky on any day of the summer or any other season. She wondered if he had, indeed, married another. After what they had shared, or her own misinterpretation of what they had shared, and his reaction to her admission of love, Gertie did not know if he was capable of ever falling in love, or if it was just that he could not love *her*. But she had been in love since then. Gertie had loved, and had been loved. They were not the same thing. She knew what love was.

Gertie was brought out of her reverie by the strong, American voice of Chester the Sailor.

"May I have this dance?"

Gertie's heart leapt into her throat. Partly, the shock came because she was not used to hearing an American accent, and she was partly surprised, because she'd been doing it again-- gazing off into the distance, pondering that boy back home. But this was not Billy Ray's music. This was Gertie's tune. She lifted her chin, and smiled into the blue, almost oceanic blue eyes of the American sailor, and raised her hand, so he could lead her out to the makeshift dance floor, which was really the hardened portion of sand between torches reserved, tonight, for dancing. As Chester the Sailor held her politely and they swayed to the island music, Gertie continued to smile, while wondering about Billy Ray. What was he doing tonight? Is he married now? Does he have children? Slowly, then all at once, her mind wrapped around acceptance. Oh, probably. Billy Ray is *such* a loving and effervescent soul that Gertie could not imagine him without the perfect life she was dreaming up for him, and it hurt her a little.

In the morning, Gertie's hut was nearly shaken down by excited children.

"Ship! Ship!"

Gertie rose and went out to the beach to see what could be the matter. Indeed, yesterday's visitor, the ship, was abuzz with activity. Sailors climbed up ladders and down ropes, inspecting every inch of the vessel, and stacking boxes on the sand. Gertie furrowed her brow and gestured to the children to stay where they stood. She began down beach toward the blue steel behemoth. A presence at her left shoulder gave her pause. Papa Datun was next to her. Gertie smiled and nodded. Papa Datun stepped slightly ahead of her. He felt protective of Gertrude, and while investigating this sea vessel, he would take the lead as a father figure.

As they approached the ship, an officer stepped forward to meet them. The sailors continued their work, rubbing the steel to a shiny sheen.

"Kalla Mara," greeted the captain.

Papa Datun embraced Captain Georgios with a shout of laughter.

As fate would have it, Papa Datun and Captain Georgios worked together on the docks of Melbourne, Australia, before Datun and Dayo left for the northern seas and Georgios' parents took him to Greece for higher learning. Georgios had attended university in Athens, then served in the navy during the War. A seafaring man never truly gets his land legs, so he stayed on the water. Papa Datun was so happy to see his old friend, and told him of Gertrude's time on the island.

"America?" Captain Georgios asked. "You are a long, long way from home."

"I feel it," Gertie agreed, her eyes filling with tears and falling to the ground.

"Brave girl," Georgios smiled. "We can get you closer. We are going to the west. We don't need an English instructor on my ship, but Jason requires assistance in the cookery."

And so it was settled. Gertie would be a kitchen assistant. She knew how to cook for a bunch of men. After all, she had grown up on a farm, for the last many years without a mother, and had cooked for her father and brothers as they planted, harvested, milked and butchered cows. And to only be an assistant! Praise be to God she did not have to do this all by herself!

Gertie did not mind being the only woman on a ship of lonely men. They catered to her every whim and wish, which was fun for a while. Captain Georgios had given strict orders that the men were to treat the female guest as they would their own sister. This was the perfect arrangement, as Gertie was nearly dying of loneliness for her brothers back home on the farm. She had plenty of privacy in her small quarters, off the kitchen, and the sailors were all very friendly, but respectful of her.

Eventually, the ship got to her, with its nearly constant whistles and alarm bells. She got very little sleep, and found herself rising to the ranks of assistant head cook. Managing young sailors turned out to be something of a A ship is a very confined place, especially for a young lady who is accustomed to wide open spaces. Gertrude began recounting in her mind all of the days at sea that she had seen in the last two years. She now longed for trees, and seas of prairie grass. She wanted to pet animals and walk on solid ground. When the ship met upon Africa, Gertrude was thrilled to touch land again, land without waves. She wanted to walk on ground that did not give beneath her feet.

Captain Georgios offered Gertie a rare opportunity — the ship would dock here, in The Sudan, until tomorrow. They were on the Red Sea. The ship would set sail again tomorrow through the canal that leads to the Mediterranean Sea, and on to Greece. It was his homeland. While here, on African soil, there were things to see. Would she like an adventure?

Gertie looked at Captain Georgios with some curiosity. She thought of Blair Corey, offering her an adventure. She thought of Tyler, and his dreams of adventure. Captain Georgios was so very much like an uncle to her, much like Papa Datun and Uncle Dayo, and he had had all of the sailors treating her like—well, like the Dairy Princess. They didn't even know they had royalty on the ship.

"What adventures await in the desert?" asked Gertie. "It doesn't look very adventurous from the dock."

And before she had finished speaking, a trumpet sounded. Perhaps, no, that wasn't a trumpet, but a beast the likes Gertie had never seen ambled up to the ship. An elephant, wearing some kind of adornments and a blanket on his (her?) back approached them, with two men on either side.

"Come," said Captain Georgios. "Let us see what beauty Africa can show us."

With this, he easily mounted the pachyderm, motioning to Gertie to join him. Gertie had ridden horses. She had managed to break the meanest of bulls on the farm in her teen years. This was an experience she was not going to forgo.

The elephant ride took Gertie and Captain Georgios into a treed area of the landscape. Along the way, Gertie saw more vegetation and animals she had never imagined. She would have to write this all down to tell Pa. He would be interested in how these folks kept their animals, or how they didn't keep them. Everything here seemed to roam wild and free, like those deer that jump like big, graceful frogs. What were they? Gazelles, Captain Georgios told her.

The elephant seemed to know where she was going. She took them to a small village, and sidled right up to a landing, where Captain Georgios and Gertie could dismount safely. It was only then that Gertie saw a smaller elephant had been behind them the whole time, carrying the handlers. These men promptly tied both elephants, while Gertie and the captain descended the stairs of the platform to dine at a nearby tent.

There were many pleasant smells, meat was smoking on outdoor fires. Gertie was unable to tell what animals she was tasting, but agreed they were delicious. There seemed to be no hurry here, much like on the island. Some people were eating, some were walking between tents, and some did not appear to have a purpose at all.

"What are you thinking about?" Captain Georgios asked her, clearly observing her watching activity.

"I wonder how the people here live," Gertie admitted. "I wonder how they work. I wonder who farms and who sells vegetables. Who teaches the children? Who makes these decisions?"

"Such worldly observations," Captain Georgios smirked. "One would think you have been doing this your entire young life. Who grows the food where you are from? Who sells the food? Who teaches? Who gets to decide?"

Gertie thought about that for a moment before answering. While sitting in U.S. History class that sunny afternoon, so long ago, she had given a fleeting thought to her future, but here, it seemed a life's role was fallen into. Back home in America, any child could choose what they would be.

"We do," Gertie offered, first quietly. "My father grows wheat. Many of my friends have chosen to become teachers, or lawyers, or businessmen. Some stay on the farm. We decide our future."

And then, out of her mouth and into her ears were the words Gertie needed to hear.

Captain Georgios nodded. "Yes, Gertrude. Your journey has taught you well."

They climbed the stairs back to the landing, and again mounted the elephant. This time, in the afternoon sun, Gertie was thankful for the animal's gigantic flapping ears, which created an intermittent breeze.

On the return trip to the dock, more creatures presented themselves to Gertie, and she could not wait to tell Zach about the striped horses and jumping deer with long antlers that somehow made it into Noah's Ark.

The Averoff glistened in the falling sun as the captain and Gertie returned. The sailors had certainly been busy today! Gertie disembarked the elephant and as she did so, patted and rubbed the face of this new friend.

"Thank you," she said. She received a blink in return, and she took that as, "You're welcome."

Gertie hurried off to the mess hall to make sure her cooks were operating on all cylinders, even without her there.

After the evening meal, Captain Georgios commanded the attention of the sailors. A teacher would be joining them on deck, and he wanted a full formation.

Captain Georgios was like that. Greeks want to know everything, and if given the opportunity to seek a teacher, they will learn. The African teacher boarded the ship, and honored the captain and officers with a pipe. The men shared the pipe, and the teacher asked the group a question, which, after some translation and gesturing, she understood to mean, "Did you give joy? Did you receive joy?"

Gertie considered this. In her childhood, life on the farm had been hard-- there were play times with her brothers, no doubt about it, but overall, given the work and worry over her mother's illness and death, and how lonesome her father was after that, life was hard. Not to mention, seasonal farming in a harsh land like North Dakota is not always straightforward. It's not for the weak of heart. But the beautiful spring, summer and fall made that Old Man Winter worth it, Gertie concluded. It forces us to plan. It emboldens us and makes us strong. She decided that it was because of those very harsh winters and that horrible, soul-wracking sobbing when her mother passed away that she was able to dance on the other end of the metaphorical spectrum. She was able to feel joy.

Then, Gertie smiled, thinking about those island children on Palau. She had shared with them English and German, to help bridge their communication gaps with their grandparents. She played beach games with them. Laughed until they could all laugh no more. Gertie felt the warm glow in her chest catch her breath and give way to an eclipsing smile, in spite of a cool Sahara evening that was black as pitch, and really sort of terrified her. Gertie strongly disliked nighttime on the desert, because it was so dark and dangerous, and the predatory animals crept near to infiltrate camp, searching for scraps of dinner or sleeping breakfast. A caravan would be leaving soon, to transport the small elephant, zebras and monkeys to a boat that would carry them to their destiny. Gertie would travel along, and see where this took her. Gertie typically did not rest much at night, but this evening, this night, after this evening's lesson from the elder, she reflected on her many previous months and travels, and was calmer. She had given joy.

9

It was always the wind. Everywhere, there was wind, Gertie thought. In Athens, Greece, it was just *windier* than other places she had been lately. Captain Georgios had talked her through Europe. He would not hear of her circling the globe, as she had, and not seeing his beloved Acropolis. After the war, there was suspicious activity elsewhere in Europe, but the captain told Gertie if she caught a train to France and a steamer to New York, she would be just fine. She was a smart girl, and after all, had made it this far. His only warning? Stay out of Germany. That broke her heart a little, because Germany is what she wanted to see. She wanted to sing in the hills of her forefathers. She wanted to listen to this wind in her grandmother's memory. But she would obey. Now, standing beneath the marble columns of the Parthenon, looking out over the sea, and knowing this structure had stood in this wind for perhaps two thousand years or more, Gertie felt her eyes moisten. She understood why Captain Georgios wanted her to experience this place. This was his home. The wind blows over Pa's fields, too, she thought, and no one ever warned her to be careful, or to "not go" somewhere. This was beautiful. That was her own home. How long would it take to get there?

Gertie detrained in Marseille, stepping down onto the train platform, a chic pump peeking out from beneath her black trench coat. The foggy French forenoon made her smirk to herself, as she tugged at a pincurl sticking out of her poke bonnet and pulled her collar up around the back of her neck to keep out the morning chill and drizzle.

If they could see me now, Gertie thought. The Dairy Princess in France! She mused if the fashionable French even kept cows. They must, she decided. How else would they get chocolate and cheese?

Gertie was used to people looking at her by now-- women's short, nondescript, but not completely unfriendly glances, and men's long, approving looks. Children always liked her. She always visited with children, in all of her travels. Maybe she would be a teacher, after all. She would be a traveling teacher. That would be fun. Then she would not have to be tied down to a dairy farm and milking those cows *every* sunrise and every night, and she would be able to see all of the world. She had gotten to a lot of it already, but there was so much more to be breathed in; there were so many people to meet, poems to write. For one scarce moment, her mind drifted to the ill-fated Tyler Texas, Cowboy Poet. That snowy mountain pass and that sickly steam engine seemed like a lifetime ago. Could it only have been last summer?

Gertie smiled and made her way to the ticket counter. She knew that there, she would find some information, pertaining to where a girl her age could go and what she might find for adventure in France, and hopefully all this would come to her in her Mother Tongue. While sailing around the world with the Greeks, Gertie had picked up some phrases, but she did not quite trust her conversational French just yet. She stood politely in line, gathering situational awareness of Marseille so far. On the other side of the depot, she could hear the deep, foggy honking of the ships. Gertrude knew she was near the water, and that brought a smile to the corners of her mouth. She thought perhaps for a moment that Marseille and Seattle were not so far apart. If she threw a stone with all her might, she just may toss it over the Purple Mountain Majesty, and it would land in her Pop's fields, and Zach would look up and know his baby sister was on her way home. Oh, wouldn't they have a good time then? But, no, Gertie raised her eyes and noted that in France, all of the French people really do wear those berets cocked to one side of their head, and that placed her still very far from home.

"When you're tired, you can sleep," Mama would say. "When you're hungry, you can eat. But when you're homesick, there is absolutely nothing to be done about it."

As she became more aware of her surroundings, and that she was still very far from home, Gertrude decided to do something about it.

Gertie awoke in her hotel room, a foggy sun peering through the window of the quarters, decorated in maritime, not unlike the rest of Marseille. She stretched, stood, and got dressed. Once her curls were pulled back and her face washed, she felt awake. Now, she could go downstairs to the hotel's breakfast room and meet people, and find out what today's adventure would entail.

From Gertrude's childhood, she'd drunk coffee. Coffee, mixed with a lot of milk and some sugar, was what she'd had for breakfast and afternoon social hour every day with her mother and the ladies. There wasn't much coffee available on Palau. She had drunk tea with the islanders during those months while she taught the children English and German, and learned more about the tropical plants that grew on the island.

In France, Gertie learned, one must drink strong, thick coffee. Espresso, they called it. In the café, the girl sweetened the cup a very little bit, making it more palatable, and added a small bit of milk and a spoon of foam to the top of the coffee in the dainty mug. With the first sip, Gertie wrinkled her nose and pursed her lips. It tasted like mud! Mud with foam! And sugar! A couple sitting at the small round table for two in front of the window noted her distinct displeasure and mademoiselle stifled a giggle, while monsieur chuckled, in spite of himself. Gertie caught them watching her. Even the poodle on the young woman's lap seemed offended at her faux pas. She straightened back up and smiled.

By the bottom of the cup, Gertie asked for a refill. She figured if she was going to learn French, a café on a marginally sunny day in Marseille was one of the best places to do it.

Anna was her new friend's name, and they chatted the morning away, making room for English and French to meet in the sentence fragments between laughter and hand gestures. Anna's boyfriend had long-since abandoned her at the café, after smiling, chuckling, and rolling his eyes were all he had to contribute to this girls-only conversation. Gertie told Anna that her frock was fetching. She learned Anna had designed it all by herself. Anna loved Gertie's hat and shoes.

They had come from a boutique in Seattle, or Japan, or maybe Thailand. But no, was it? Gertie was beginning to think she should write some of this down. It had been a long time since she had a girlfriend with whom she could delve into stories, and retelling her last year could take forever. She just knew she was missing important parts and pieces, but hoped Anna didn't mind. Anna's English wasn't all that good at the moment, and Gertie was mostly thinking to herself that she would have to tell this story again when she gets home to North Dakota one day, and her father will not want one minute detail left out. She should decide what to edit before that story-telling session occurs, in the interest of believability. There are certain things a father doesn't need to hear.

After three or four cups of cappuccino, the girls decided to go for a walk.

Anna learned that Gertie loved animals and flowers, and Gertie learned that Anna loved to sew and dance. In fact, there was a dance tonight, she gathered, and Anna would get her something to wear for going out. She invited Gertie to her home, and they were so busy walking and talking up a storm, and without really accepting the invitation, Gertie suddenly found herself being led through a gate in a picket fence, into a front yard garden that smelled wonderful, and very familiar. She paused. She breathed in, and closed her eyes. She smiled. She felt her mother here. There were roses and tulips, lavender and butterflies. Gertie thought she saw a big, fat bumble bee meander past her nose, but she couldn't be sure, such was the wonder of it all. Her left hand played at the cameo pin on her lapel, which held the family picture of her parents, her brothers, and herself. This garden's perfume smelled like home.

Gertie realized, there she'd gone, thinking again, and Anna was already up on the porch, looking back at her, with a half-smile. The past thirty seconds felt like several minutes.

"Did I lose you, Gertie?" Anna asked. "Are you tired?"

"No, no, this garden is so beautiful," Gertie started. But she wasn't able to finish, because Anna had swung wide the front door, and was calling for her mother. The smell of fresh bread wafted from the kitchen by the time Gertie arrived inside the front door, and her stomach growled approvingly.

Anna's mother was a pleasantly plump woman, and every surface, corner, and crevice of her kitchen was covered with croissants, croutons, and buttery baguettes. She motioned for Gertie to sit at the prominent chair in the middle of the kitchen, and no sooner had Gertie's muscles relaxed into the seat, were a cup of coffee and a croissant in front of her.

Anna's mother was Eve, and she tried to speak to Gertie in English, and Gertie tried to communicate just as respectfully in French, but Anna gracefully interceded. Eve wanted to know from where Gertrude had come, by what path, and where she had family. It was just a sin in her eyes that a sweet girl such as herself was so far away from her family. Eve wiped tears from her eyes while saying something in French that Gertie guessed meant she should go home.

When the coffee cups were emptied, Anna pulled on Gertie's sleeve, and they went to Anna's room. There, Gertie was transported to the pictures in the Vogue magazine back home on her pink bedroom floor. Feather boas and crystal light fixtures dripped from the ceiling, casting light bubbles across the walls and floor. Gertrude thought, looking at this room, that she had entered the princess' chambers, and she was in the presence of royalty.

"I like beautiful things," Anna laughed, in a way that made her words curl and dance around the room, and up to the light and boas on the walls and ceiling. "Let me show you."

Opening the closet door, Anna opened a whole new world to Gertrude. It was a world of dresses, shoes, hats, gloves, finery not seen back home or anywhere she'd been, and she had been around the world.

"Anna! What is all this?" Gertie was in complete wonderment.

"This," Anna spoke softly. "This is my world."

She made clothes. Anna thought about what her mother might like to wear to the market, and she sewed it. Then, she would dream up flapper dresses. During this process, she would consider dressing men as well. Someone had to dance with the flappers. Dapper mannequins gazed out the window in Anna's elegant chamber. They looked lonely. Gertie caught herself, worrying about the mental state of mannequins, and elected instead to try on a green flapper dress.

In the midst of the music and laughter, and flapping her arms up and down, down and up, like a bird in a puddle of rain, everything became quite like slow motion to Gertie, and she smiled to herself. Dancing, here, in France, to the American jazz music, was like the world of the magazines had jumped up from her bedroom floor and collided. She had lived lifetimes from a year ago, and she would see many more. She would dance many dances. Sing many lullabies. Sunsets and sunrises would be sweeter and brighter because of the trumpets crying out to her tonight. She wasn't where she'd been. She wasn't where she was going yet. But this journey had taken such a turn, so quickly, Gertie thought. *You just never knew what to expect.*

The music changed, as Gertie whirled out into the night and into the arms of a stranger. She did not flap or jump, jive or wail. For a few tender moments, she let herself relax in the comfortable, strong arms of a capable dance partner, in the bright moonlight, as the brass players cried out to the stars. Gertie fantasized she could, perhaps, stay here forever, in France, swaying to the sweet song of the trumpets and the bones, but the tiny raindrops decided a different fate for her. Far off, Anna was calling her name, and it was time to go home.

"Gertie!" Anna exclaimed. Anna's eyes were wet with not only rain, but it looked like tears as well, which tore Gertie away from the stranger as Anna tugged on her sleeve. "Gertie, come on. Come with me. Come with me now."

The two young women ran away down the cobblestone streets, in the direction of Anna's house.

"What happened, Anna?" Gertie was chasing her, trying to catch up, wearing shoes, to which she was not accustomed, and after dancing in them all night, her feet were especially sore.

"He danced with her," Anna was crying. "He danced with another girl. He is kissing her now!" But she was exclaiming out into the night, completely exhausting herself with every outcry, and Gertie was only catching every other word. "He doesn't love me. He said he doesn't love me."

Ah, thought Gertie, this, this is an area of her expertise.

Anna's boyfriend from the cafe` was back there now, in the midst of the music, wrapped in an embrace with someone who was not Anna. This is where she might help-- affairs of the heart, and rascally men. This is why God brought her here, to Anna, to assist in the healing of a heart.

"Wait, wait, be calm. Let him consider what he is losing," Gertie suggested gently. "Don't let him see you for a while. He'll come around soon enough. Or, he won't, and then you'll know you're truly better off without him."

The girls reached the front door garden, and Anna stopped. She turned around, and stared Gertie dead in the eye, as she wiped rain and tears from her own.

"Don't tell my mother," Anna deadpanned. "She's not well, and she thinks we're getting married. This news would surely kill her. You have to help me keep up the charade."

Gertie agreed, even though it sounded a little strange. She could not imagine that robust woman inside this house being anything but completely healthy, and genuinely felt affection for her, but did not want to be the one to send her to the grave.

The two young women stayed awake into the early morning hours, alternately crying and giggling like much younger schoolgirls about all the things girls do-- boys and clothes, and what their lives would be. Later in the day, whatever time it was, probably around noon, Gertie caught a wafting smell of coffee and the beginning of bread. She heard the rumble in her stomach, and realized, after expending so much energy on the dance floor and laughing into the night, Gertie was very hungry.

"Pssst. Anna," she hissed.

A faint moan came from the other bed as the lump under the covers began to move. A creature unbecoming of Gertie's friend from the previous day emerged, and its green eyes met hers.

"Hungry," the creature muttered. "Café."

"I know," agreed Gertie. "Let's go see what's downstairs. Mmm, I smell coffee." Stretching, the two girls yawned, slowly got out of their beds, donned bright, sunny day dresses, and descended the kitchen steps.

Still rubbing the sleep from her eyes, Anna encountered what would be the most disturbing scene of her life. There, on the kitchen floor, lay her mother, passed out cold. Momentary shock stopped her dead in her tracks. Anna couldn't scream. She could not cry out. She was not able to gasp in fear, despair, or for help. Her mother had begun baking this morning, and dough was rising all over the kitchen, ready to be baked into all forms of bread, rolls, croissants, and croutons in the enormous brick oven. Hot coffee was waiting on the fiery stove. In no time, Anna was on the floor, at her mother's side, softly tapping her cheek to wake her. She was nonplussed.

Without a word, Gertie slid an oven glove onto her hand, picked the coffee pot up and set it down on a metal holder away from the fire. She checked the oven, and, still, without saying anything to her worried friend, began filling it with the various forms of dough. Otherwise, it would go to waste, and it would be a sin for Eve to work so hard for nothing. She figured, a kitchen was a kitchen, and with some investigating, most things were in the same places in most kitchens. She could be of some help. Anna was still tending to her mama, and she still was getting no response.

Soon the oven was filled, the kitchen put into reasonable order, coffee cups filled for Gertie and for Anna, Anna looked up at her friend.

"Thank you," Anna said in a half-whimper, half-whisper.

"I just wanted to make it easier," Gertie offered. "I wanted to try to do my part. She was so kind to me. "

Anna's mother was gone. Gertie was sure of this. She had died.

"I'm going to go next door over to bring back help," Gertie offered. "Stay here. Stay calm. I'll be right back."

No, Anna got herself together enough in front of her friend to say she would go to the neighbor. Gertie looked down at Anna, knowing exactly the state she was in, after losing her own mother, after feeling the world drop out from beneath her own feet and having nothing to hold onto, she said no. Gertie told Anna she should not be doing that in the state she was, and she got Anna to agree to sit, just drink some coffee and try not to cause any trouble. That last request brought a short smile to Anna's face. Gertie asked her to watch the oven, for it was full of Madame's bread.

As Gertie closed the front door of the house and descended the steps, her chest heaving and her jaw tight, she concurrently felt the irony. She talked Anna down from a temper tantrum last night over a man whose attentions were easily swayed, and now, having experience in the arena of dying mothers, she would be there for her new friend. She would help with this transition.

As she stepped carefully, trying to think of what she would say, she reminded herself to breathe. She was very sad for Anna, her new friend who did not seem to have any other family but her darling mother, darling Madame Morrelle, who whirled around her kitchen creating wonderment and hospitality. What would Anna do now?

Gertie found herself knocking timidly at the door of a cottage not far away. A small man with spectacles perched at the tip of his nose opened the door wide and invited her inside.

"Please come," Gertie pleaded. "Madame Morrelle. Please come."

Knowing the man may, or may not, comprehend whatever she just said, Gertie said no more. She grasped hold of the neighbor's forearm and yanked him along with her, back to Chateau de Morrelle. He sputtered in surprise, and the spectacle of a young woman pulling Monsieur Phillipe across the yard stopped the morning bustle.

When they stepped into Madame Morrelle's kitchen, Anna was wailing. She was pleading, in French, with her mother to awaken, to stand, to have morning coffee with her.

Gertie took Anna by the shoulders, then around the waist, to forcibly pull her friend away from the departed soul's shell on the floor. Anna's mother was no longer there. Monsieur Phillipe examined her.

"Get a sheet," he told the girls, without turning around. By now, Armando, the yardman, had come in, and not a moment too soon. Armando was a giant of a man, and was family to everyone in the neighborhood. Rumor had it that he had served on a ship when he was young, but now he spent his days, visiting the neighbors, helping with tasks that needed to be done. Armando sized up the situation on the floor of the kitchen, dropped to one knee, and offered a prayer up to God, all before Monsieur Phillipe informed him of anything.

When he stood, Armando and Monsieur Phillipe spoke quietly. Anna was beginning to retreat into herself, Gertie surmised. She watched the tears dry on her friend's face, and her jaw set. She wondered what was happening below that surface. In Gertie's mind, life was so fleeting. Every moment should be savored, enjoyed. Her own mother's death taught her to see the beauty in everything, and see everything she could. Seeing Anna's mother leave this quickly, Gertie was learning a different lesson: Family is everything. What would Anna do now? Of course it wasn't as if she was a child, with childish needs, requiring a mother to tend to every whim and whisper, but Anna needed her mother to keep her even. Anna was a bit of a butterfly soul. Her mother made sure she still ate and slept, and both at the appropriate times of day or night.

Monsieur Phillipe stood. He and Armando, as gently as a newborn, swathed Madame Morrelle in the sheet, and Armando carried her toward the door.

"Where are you taking her?" Anna demanded, new tears now whipping off of her cheekbones.

Monsieur Phillipe hushed her gently, while placing his hands on each of Anna's shoulders so she wouldn't rush forward and knock Armando down, with Madame's body in his arms. He explained to Anna that Armando had a cabinet built that may suffice as a casket, for the purpose of laying her mother to rest. Anna and her mother did not have anyone else in the world but Phillipe and Armando. They were family, as far as family goes, and they would share blood, if blood could be shared. Phillipe would do anything for Madame Morrelle's daughter, for he felt Anna was his own flesh and blood.

Can this be happening? Anna's mind was racing. *What will happen now?* She did not realize the words were tumbling out of her mouth over and over, repeating themselves in French, then English, then French again. Her mother's departure from this earth took her so by surprise, that any plans she might have made were now null and void.

Gertrude believed her role here, to be the supportive friend Anna needed, was to make everything as easy as possible. She filled coffee cups. She set out plates of baguettes and butter on the table. She knew discussions were coming. Gertie did not know how funeral proceedings were done in France, but she assumed they were much the same as in North Dakota, where everything begins with a cup of coffee and good bread. She smiled to herself as she thought it was considerate and compassionate of Madame Morrelle to make fresh croissants this morning. Anna's mother was always the lovely caretaker, making every room nicer just by being in it. Even now, there were fresh flowers on the table.

It was a lovely, sunny day in France, and the pink and white roses were blooming mercifully out in the garden where Anna and Gertie lounged. Anna still had some tears left, but she was nearly cried out. She could not wail anymore. The day they buried her mother was a rainy, cold day.

Do you know why our garden is so messy? Anna asked. It's a fractal. It's beautiful and complex, yet simple in its reasoning. It's like a person.

Gertie thought about her best friend, this garden of many colors was a perfect representation. Anna was, herself, beautiful and complex. Her relationships were hard and dramatic. She loved with all she had in her heart. And she left with all she could when they were over.

In the days that followed the burial, Anna became very emptied of all emotion. Gertie helped her best friend clean the cottage, which had always been ample for Anna and her mother. They gave the enormous supply of baked goods, canned fruits and vegetables, to Armando and Phillipe, for Anna had decided she was leaving this house. She would never again spend a holiday here, that it would smell of the cinnamon twists her mother never failed to make for Christmas morning. She could not dream of awakening on her birthday morning without her mother's ceremonious entrance into her chamber with a breakfast tray, holding all Anna's favorite treats. Heaven was just too far away, and Anna could not stay here. This house was too close to the pain.

"My life is over," Anna wailed into her forearms. "I don't know what to do now. My mother is gone. She's gone, gone. She's not alive, anywhere. Now what do I do?"

Gertie watched as Anna screamed and cried, hair everywhere, knowing this was coming from somewhere within and she had to get out of her body. Gertie knew exactly how this felt, to lose a mother, to feel like there is nothing left in the world to hold onto, and she chose her next words carefully.

"You're my best friend, Anna," Gertie began very calmly. "You are like a sister to me. Come to America. Come to North Dakota. I will share my family with you. You will love my father and brothers. We have plenty of room in the house, and there are animals, and plenty of jobs to do. You'll be able to get a job. You could even get seamstress work."

Anna looked up from her tear-stained arms, her face red with emotion.

"Really?" she asked. "I could sew in America?"

Gertie burst into laughter, which she really could not contain, this being a rather inappropriate time to be laughing at her distraught friend, whose life was really decimated with a relationship breakup, the death of her mother, and uncertainty of the future. She just couldn't help it.

"They would be thrilled to have you sew there!" Gertie exclaimed, her voice lilting with laughter. "Did I ever tell you about the awful purple shirt I tried to make for my brother? He made me promise to never pick up a needle and thread again!"

For the first time in days, Anna smiled. She even laughed.

"You mean, we have found something you cannot do? You cannot sew? But it is so easy! A straight line! All you have to do is pay attention, Gertrude! Can you not do that?" Anna would probably enjoy this superiority for a while, and Gertie was happy to momentarily cheer her up.

The girls bought their passage aboard the ocean liner, set to leave from Versailles on Tuesday. Now, continued the process of closing up Anna's life in France. Armando was of immense assistance in selling furniture, and Anna's mother's clothing. What couldn't be sold was donated to the poor. Armando would handle the cottage for her. Anna may want to return one day, Armando told her, and she would need a home. He would keep the house up for her.

Armando drove Gertie and Anna to the docks for boarding. To see the parting of Armando and Anna made Gertude even more lonesome for her father. Armando teared up, said something beautiful in French, and Anna promised to write. She was going to America after all. Everyone wanted to go to America!

Through her tears, Anna smiled, "Armando, you must sail with us."

"Ah, my heart," Armando replied, "you go first. Write to me, and I will come later."

He unloaded the trunks, and the dockhands took the luggage from him. After much ado, Gertie and Anna entered into their new adventures.

10

In New York City, there were Germans. There were French. There were Palauans. There were Japanese. Gertie and Anna happened upon a Greek luncheonette, and Anna's eyes locked with the green eyes of a Greek man. Yes, a Greek. From that moment on, Gertie was not sure if her personal costume maker would ever make it to North Dakota.

"Gertrude, I'm in love. Love!" Anna whirled about in such glee, the pangs of slight jealousy Gertie had been harboring since her breakup with Billy Ray really were faint.

"I'm happy, Anna," Gertie told her. "I honestly am happy for you. Are you coming on the western train?"

"Even better!" Anna's eyes glinted with a spark Gertie had never seen since the day in France when they played dress-up and went out on the town as flapper girls.

"Peter has spoken with his uncle. He will be boarding the train! He is coming along! We will get married!"

Gertie smiled, at the glee Anna was exuding, even if this was happening dramatically fast. These were fast-moving times. This was good news. Who knew what tomorrow held? Anna would have a family, hope, and a future. All of these were things that Anna's mother would have wanted for her, Gertie smiled to herself.

It was agreed that Gertie would go ahead to North Dakota, and Anna would come later, perhaps in a week or two, with Peter. There had been no news from the middle of the country, so the friends made their plans without knowing of the weather events taking place.

11

The train service stopped at Fargo, due to flooding conditions out west. There was a brave set of souls gathering up a train of Ford Model As to roll out to Bismarck. These were hardy Dakotans, men who could get through any kind of weather, and were betting their boots they could get through a flood.

Gertie's trunk was loaded onto the rumble seat of a 1929 Model A at sunrise. The sojourners camped out at Spiritwood that night. It didn't look good the next morning. This being a new state, these spring waters were rising higher and higher, but everyone knew that the snow would melt. They just didn't know how far they would have to go to get away from it all. Gertie knew this kind of water didn't happen at home, and home was where she was headed.

The next morning, they started off again away from the

sunrise. Some of the Model As were having trouble, due to the saturated soil through which they tread. Soil failure is not obvious, until the dirt is depended upon. Suddenly, a hill may give way, and it is found that the water table has risen.

The men stopped driving at Sterling to discuss the situation and how to proceed.

"The wheels are getting tired," Floyd shook his head. "Our load is heavy on these automobiles. We are going to have to lighten. What can we do?"

The group came upon a trail of horse-drawn wagons. It seemed that the horses knew a bit better than the new automobiles, and could get around the muck.

Gertie looked around the prairie in despair. She was so close to home, had traversed oceans, and now a little mud was going to keep her away? Not today.

"Sir? Sir! Mr. Davis!" Gertie recognized a farmer adjusting his team of horses.

"Well, if it isn't Trudybelle, the Legacy Dairy Princess," Mr. Davis chuckled. "How are you young lady? Quite the thing we've got going on here."

"Mr. Davis," Gertie began. "I have got to get home, and…"

"Well, I can get you to Mandan," Mr. Davis interrupted her. "Let's get your things in the box. With that, he handily retrieved her steamer trunk from the rumble seat of the Model A. She gestured thanks to the driver and swung up into the wagon seat next to Mr. Davis, the cattle commissioner.

Gertie felt safe, for the first time in many, many months, perhaps in a few years. Mr. Davis knew who she was and knew her family. She was starting to feel normal. The ride in the wagon was sloppy, thanks to the water table, but the scenery was absolutely stunning, thought Gertie. It was her beautiful, breathtaking North Dakota. The horses did very well with what they had to go on. Not only did Mr. Davis drive Gertie to Mandan, but he had to see a man about a herd in Judson, so Gertie assured him she could walk to the farm from there. It was only a few miles.

Gertie winced as another blister on her left foot cracked, and she just knew it was bleeding. She didn't have a choice. She'd broken her heel some time ago, and dragging her trunk for the last eleven miles had done nothing good to her back, her legs, or her disposition.

Gertrude could see herself, in her mind's eye. She was a mess. There would be no county fair queen contests today. She was covered in dried mud. The floodwaters had never reached this part of Dakota, and with every step she took, Gertie could feel the ground was returning to dust beneath her feet.

***

Zachary was mending a fence out on the main road. If he was ever going to convince Peggy to marry him and move out here, he had to get this place into shape, and keeping the cows in would make less work for him in the long run. Out of the corner of his eye, Zach saw something limping up the section line toward the main road about a quarter away. Was it an animal? He squinted. Whatever kind of animal drags a box around? Looks like one of those big suitcases they take on ships. Zach's eyes widened. He dropped his fencing hammer and ran. He ran that quarter-mile faster than he ever had before. Gasping and laughing, there was his baby sister! He picked Gertie up and swung her around, both of them crying and laughing, and laughing and crying. When Zach set her back down and got a look at her, he could see that Gertie had been through something of an ordeal. He picked up her steamer trunk.

"Come on," Zach said. "Christopher's in the barn."

Fifty yards from the farm, Zach whistled. Bewildered, Christopher wandered out of the barn, and broke into a run to embrace Gertie.

"Where's Pa?" Gertie asked. "She was out of breath from laughing, being hugged so tightly, and dragging her steamer trunk eleven miles.

"Let's go for a ride," Zach suggested. Christopher helped Gertie into the wagon with the team already hitched up, and climbed up on the other side of her.

"It is a real blessing to see your face again, sister," Christopher told her.

"I tried to write," Gertie began.

Zach interrupted her.

"You're here now. Most important thing."

He turned off of Route 10, into the Graceland Cemetery. Gertie looked around, assuming Pa was visiting Mama's grave. The wagon rolled to a stop and the trio dismounted. With a brother on either side of her, Gertie approached her mama's grave.

"I'm home, Mama," she told the headstone. Zach and Christopher shared a glance. Then, Gertie's realization was almost as if she was dreaming. Together in their final resting place, their parents now lay. The headstone reflected their father's name, as well. The sickness last winter had been so terrible.

"Pa?" Gertie was shaking her head, eyes wide in disbelief, tears falling from her face. Zach wrapped her in a protective hug, and Christopher put his hands on both of their shoulders. They were orphans now. Full-grown orphans.

Gertie's love for her parents rushed through her mind and memory like a waterfall. She had been so fortunate to be so loved by such caring, nurturing people. She thought of the parents on the island, and how they take care of all of the children, not only their own. Gertie pondered of the kindness of Uncle Dayo, Monsieur Phillipe and Madame Morrelle, and their parental ways, even though they did not know her well, they were kind to her. She, in turn, had been there with Anna during the mourning of her mother. Life is round, she thought. We all do what we can to help each other through it.

12

Gertie set about the business of getting settled back in at home. She would start working at the café, and drop in on Mary, to see how she was enjoying teaching and married life.

As his little sister was hanging her washing on the line, Zach came back from town with news. He informed Gertie that Billy Ray was in jail for moonshine. This news made Gertie's heart swell. Jail? What if he's cold? What if he's hungry? Zach didn't care. It seems he rather hoped Billy Ray was both cold and hungry, for the breaking of Gertie's heart, which resulted in her absence from their lives for so long. Gertie said she would have to think about that herself.

***

Gertie tightened the white lace strings on her pink gingham

apron, and wiped down another table. Miss Laurie was straightening up the dishes and cleaning the counter after the lunch folks had gone for the day. There at Schmidt's Café, they were never alone, but they were never too busy, either. Miss Laurie knew all about Gertrude's journey around the world, and she was not one bit impressed that Gertie landed back in the dusty little town from which she had originated.

"I cannot stop thinking about him," Gertie told her. "I was in paradise. I was in Paris. My heart belongs to Billy Ray, and I am sure he could care less about me. He said he didn't mind that I love him. But I love the Billy Ray he used to be, and that Billy Ray just may not be around anymore.

"Aw, hell, Gertie," Laurie began. Gertrude snapped to attention. She had been around the world, had been the only woman on a ship of cursing sailors, but when Laurie spat out that word, all Gertie could see was her sainted, Sunday school teacher mother's face, smiling sweetly at her, reminding her to be patient, and kind, and things would turn about when God was ready for them to happen.

"Why would you want to be with a man like that?" Laurie hissed. "A man who doesn't love you passionately? I've known you five minutes, and I know who you are, and what kind of man you deserve. You are everything, you deserve a man who completely wants to be with you, not a wishy-washy, can't make a decision nobody. Besides, leave him in jail. He'll dry out there, if he can't make shine or drink it all day. It's a good place for him. Is that the kind of future you want? A man who can't tell you he loves you? A man who disappoints as easily as he breathes? A man who disappears without warning? I don't think so. Not the girl I know."

Gertie nodded. She would have to think about that herself.

Howard had attended school in a neighboring town, and played baseball. He was a few years older, and he had gone to live with his uncle in Texas, a million miles away, to get his law degree. Now Howard had returned home to help his father and mother with their farm and legal affairs with the general store. Times were straining around these parts, these days. Folks needed to buy provisions, so they would walk to town with their cream buckets on Saturday, take them to the creamery, sell them for whatever they could possibly get, and that was their budget for the weekly trip to the store. It seemed few people were buying new shirts or getting haircuts for Saturday night dances anymore.

"Would you be able to help him?" Gertie asked Howard, one day while she was shopping in the store, picking up staple items like sugar and cocoa. She spied cinnamon on a shelf way up high and smiled. Howard saw the smile and knew what Gertie was thinking. He reached the cinnamon down for her and placed the container on the counter. Gertie would be baking his own mother's countywide famous cinnamon chocolate brownies, and he secretly hoped she would invite him over for them.

"I think I can recall Billy Ray," mused Howard, rubbing his clean shaven strong jaw. "Farm kid? Baseball player? Hell of an arm on that guy, right?"

He was referring to football. The Pirates had been undefeated when Gertie and Billy Ray were in high school back in their old Durham High days, and no one could win against a team with Billy Ray on it.
Howard pursed his lips, nodded to himself, then raised one eyebrow and leveled his sky blue eyes dead into Gertie's grass green globes.

"Do you want me to help him?"

"Well, I," she began. "I don't want him in jail. I don't want him in pain. I don't want anybody to hurt. I wish it were different."

"What's his sentence?" Howard asked.

"I don't know," Gertie told him. "I don't know how he's still alive. I've been gone. I heard tell of how bootleggers are killed or paralyzed or made blind by this moonshine. I don't know what he thought he was doing. I don't know what on earth he hoped to accomplish by brewing that."

"Did you ever think maybe he was bored? Or maybe depressed? Or maybe that you left, so he didn't know what to do with himself anymore, so he was trying to kill himself by making moonshine?"

Gertrude continued her diatribe. "I hardly think so. I confessed my undying love for him when we were kids. He told me he 'didn't mind' that I loved him. Didn't mind! That I loved him! So I left. I circled the planet. I saw everything, and I did it alone. The Orient! The desert! The oceans! I went all by myself. I am never going to be disregarded like that again. I don't want him to hurt. I hate that he's in the situation he's in, but I'm in a position to help him. He needs me now."

Howard was quiet for a while, as he stared out the window at the fruitless field. Gertie could tell there were a thousand things happening inside his head, so she waited for him to speak.

"Do you want to put your faith in a man like that, Gert? Let's say we get him out of jail. He goes back to moonshining, because that is what he knows. He'll get a few more folks hooked on it. That's a few more lives and families destroyed. Then what? He may get killed, or worse, he may just become blind from the 'shine, or paralyzed, from whatever he's putting in it. What about those other people in the speakeasies? What do we do for them? How many of them can we help? What about their farms? Their families? Think of the kids, Gert. What about the kids whose parents are being hurt by this man? It might be easier, and not to mention, better for society, and all of us, to leave that moonshiner in the clink to reflect on the error of his ways, Gertie."

Gertie stared at him, wide-eyed. She hadn't thought of all that. She suddenly felt very selfish. She was thankful for all of her experiences that overshadowed Billy Ray, and all of the days and times she had that were not about Billy Ray. Her travel life was about growing up, and about knowing who she was and what she wanted to do with the rest of her life. She felt like she could handle anything, anything in the world, for she had seen the world. She had seen the world without the boy Billy Ray. Billy Ray had never left home, had never evolved past his high school football victories, and his immature addictions had caught up with him and entrapped him. Gertie would not be responsible for Billy Ray hurting other people. After spending a year on Palau, learning about Southern Pacific agriculture, and how to help those island people feed their families, Gertie could not imagine allowing someone to feed others poison in the name of a good time. She knew now what she had to do. She felt convicted.

"We decide," she'd told Captain Georgios on a hot Saharan afternoon. Gertie believed it now, more than ever. *We decide what we will be.*

13

The stiff North Dakota breeze clinked the American flag against its pole as Gertie smoothed her hair back (oh drat! These unruly curls and this North Dakota wind!), and each stylish, leather shoe, alternatively, kicked and smeared as much dust as possible off of the other. She knew she looked more beautiful and more sophisticated than he had ever seen her. Gertrude's heart was pounding, so loudly she could hear it, and she was sure anyone else would be able to hear it as well. She pressed her lips together, feeling her divine red lipstick stick ever-so slightly, batted her eyelashes, to herself, believing this was the very moment she traveled around the world for. Gertie straightened her shoulders toward the door of the jail, took a deep breath and made the brave first step.

The jailer led her to a dank cell at the end of a dim hallway. A creature stirred from within.

"Company." The jailer barked and backed away, but not too far. After all, Gertie was a lady.

The shuffling prisoner made his way over to the bars, looking disinterested at best, rather unkempt and missing some teeth. Gertie wondered how that had happened. Had he gotten into a fight? She felt as though she were looking at an old man, or some kind of troll beneath a bridge. This was the unrequited love of her younger years? He just didn't look that good anymore. He was dirty, and he'd let himself fall completely apart.

"Gert?" came the recognition. This was the moment for which she had travelled around the world. He knew whom she was, and she had no desire to acknowledge him. But she'd come so far, she must.

"Billy Ray."

"Gert, you look good."

Gertie's mouth curled upward at the compliment, realizing she would never see him again after today. She laid the charm on thick.

"I won't lie to you and tell you the same, Billy Ray. You should have left the sauce alone."

Gertie could tell that her words had bite. Billy Ray winced and began coughing. The hacking wracked his body and he fell over onto the floor of his cell. This was enough, Gertie thought. She had come. She was standing here, in front of her change of heart, staring at her alternate future, silently thanking God for her youthful impetuousness, for her father's wisdom, although it had broken his heart to say goodbye to her when she got on the train with Tyler, he probably saved her life. Looking at Billy Ray, love of her childhood, Gertrude knew that had she stayed home, she would have died here. Some supernatural force had protected her all the way around the globe, and she thanked God. On the train, on the sea, in the island storms, and in the flooding, when she was almost home, she never felt like she would not get here. This man, who had given up, was a desperate soul. Gertie wondered, if that admission of love in the summer after high school graduation had been the only time anyone had told him he was loved?

Billy Ray's pa had been in trouble, Gertie remembered. When he sold off parts of the farm, that family's drinking was the talk of the town. His ma was sickly, so Billy Ray had a big responsibility. He raised himself. The most adoration he ever had was on the athletic field, or from Gertie. He wasn't good at the soft-hearted stuff, and that is how he fell so low into the gutter when the fields went dry. A whole life, Gertie thought. She looked at this man, who had been the star baseball player of their high school, the charmer, the boy with the personality to match his boisterousness. How sad, to waste a whole life… Gertie's thought trailed off into the unknown, where she would never think it again.

Gertie turned on her heel and walked back down the hall, the way she had come. She was finished here. She had seen for herself. She thought of the island children, and the light in their eyes when they understood what she was trying to teach them. It was rewarding to reach into the lives of children like that, and Gertie knew she could change the world, in her own way, if she could strive to see that light. Billy Ray's light had gone out long ago. Gertie knew what she would do, and she would do it today. She left the jail, and headed toward the school. It was one of those sunny spring days at the cusp of summer.

www.ingramcontent.com/pod-product-compliance
Lightning Source LLC
Chambersburg PA
CBHW060257150626
46556CB00021B/1895